STITCH

Satan's Fury MC

L Wilder

Stitch
Satan's Fury MC
Copyright © 2015 L Wilder
Print Edition

This book is a work of fiction. Some of the places named in the book are actual places. The names, characters, brands, and incidents are either the product of the author's imagination or are used fictitiously. The author acknowledges the trademarked status and owners of various products and locations referenced in this work of fiction, which have been used without permission. The publication or use of these trademarks is not authorized, associated with, or sponsored by the trademark owners.

Warning: This book is intended for readers 18 years or older due to bad language, violence, and explicit sex scenes.

Editor – Marci Ponce

Levi Stocke: www.facebook.com/levi.stocke

Photographer – Mariusz Jeglinski
www.facebook.com/mariusz.jeglinski
mariuszjeglinski.com

Cover design and book teasers – Monica Langley Holloway
www.facebook.com/Kustombooks2reviews
and Carrie at Cheeky Book covers
cheekycovers.com

Be sure to check out my pages: www.facebook.com/AuthorLeslieWilder

Webpage: www.lwilderbooks.com

Newsletter:
facebook.us11.list-manage.com/subscribe?u=6f10ae9ade496c2b4e3ca7a92&id=daf5289164

Amanda Faulkner PA – (my amazing PA)
www.facebook.com/BcgwMarketing

Give her a shout if you are an author in need of promoting your book. She does an amazing job.

She also runs an amazing blog:
www.facebook.com/Bookclubgonewrong

Dedication

To My Family

Thank you for being there when I needed you
the most. Your love and support has meant the
world to me.

Prologue

"HUSH, LITTLE BABY, don't say a word. Mama's gonna buy you a mockingbird. If that mockingbird don't sing, Mama's gonna buy you a diamond ring," my grandmother sang. Her voice was low and soft, and I finally started to calm down after another one of my nightmares. They started shortly after I moved in with my grandparents. I was eight years old when my parents were killed in a car crash, forcing my sister Emerson, and me to move from the only home we'd ever known to live with my father's parents. We barely knew them, but they were the only relatives we had. I never knew how good we really had it until it was all ripped away. It had almost been a year, but I was still having a hard time adjusting to the change. That night I'd made the mistake of accidentally wetting the bed. My grandmother held me close, trying to comfort me while she continued to sing. I knew her words were a lie, that my mother was dead and gone, but listening to her soothed me. "If that diamond

ring turns brass, Mama's gonna buy you a looking glass."

Pound.

Pound.

Pound.

His fist slammed against the wall as he
walked towards my room. Horror washed over
me as I listened to his footsteps coming down
the hall. The floorboards creaked under the
weight of his body, my dread intensifying with
every step he took.

Closer.

Closer.

Closer.

My head was pressed against my grandmother's chest, listening to her heart thump rapidly
while he started to shout, "Don't coddle that
boy, Louise. Stop lying to him! His mama's dead.
She can't buy him a damn thing! He's no fucking
baby. We're not raising him to be a goddamn
pussy!" he barked as he stood in the doorway
with a scowl on his face.

"George," she started, but he quickly cut her
off, raising his palm up in the air, silently ordering her to shut up. She always tried to get him to
stop, but it never worked. Once he got it in his
head, there was no changing his mind.

"Don't," she pleaded as I curled deeper into
her lap when he started stalking towards me.
With his finger pointed directly in my face, he

growled, "You wet that damn bed again, boy?" Rage vibrated off of him as he spoke, and I knew what was coming. He was furious, and only one thing happened when he got that worked up.

The barn.

My grandfather was a military man, born and bred. He still looked the part too, sporting his buzz cut and the same athletic build he had in all of his army pictures. Every minute of every day was controlled by his orders. He ran a tight ship with impossible expectations. The old man was a force to be reckoned with and he hated any sign of weakness. Which meant he detested me. He hated that I was so weak, that my parents' death still tormented me. He was determined to make a man out of me, even if that meant killing me in the process. There was a time, when the beatings first started, that he was careful, not wanting to leave any evidence of the abuse. But as I grew older, he made sure to leave the marks. He got some kind of sick satisfaction seeing the whelps on my back, smiling whenever he saw me looking at them. He wanted me to see them, to feel the raised scars on my flesh, so I would always remember. He grabbed my hand, yanking me from my grandmother's lap and snarled, "Get your ass to the barn. I'll teach you not to wet the fucking bed, boy." I could smell the mix of old spice and bourbon swirl around me as my body collided against his side.

"George, it's late," Grandmother Louise pleaded.

Ignoring her, he pulled me out of the room and down the hall. As I stumbled behind him, I caught a glimpse of Emerson sitting up in her bed, tears streaming down her chubby little cheeks. She was only four years old, but she knew what happened out in the barn. Even though it sucked that I was his main target, I was thankful that he'd never taken her out there. The old man had a soft spot for her, and she could do no wrong. I wasn't resentful. I felt the same way about her.

My bare feet dragged along in the dirt and grass as he pulled me into the barn; the large wooden doors slammed behind us, leaving us in the dark. The smell of straw and livestock whirled around me as he jerked me further into the dark. There was a time when I would try to pull away from him, but I quickly learned there was no use fighting him. I was trapped, unable to break free from his grasp. After binding my hands over my head, he reached for his favorite leather strap.

"If your father was still alive, he'd be disgusted with you. Such a fucking disappointment. You're just like your damn mother. Worthless," he grumbled as the strap whipped across my back. A searing pain shot through me, like hot coals burning through my thin t-shirt. I forced myself to hold back my cries as he continued to thrash the leather against my back, not wanting to give him the satisfaction of seeing me break. Unfortunately, that only made him angrier causing him to hit even harder. Thankfully, it didn't take long for me to pass out from the pain, my body falling limp against the restraints.

There were many more nights like that, more than I could even begin to count. At least some were quick, not like the times he'd make me wait for it. I hated those nights the most. I'd spend the whole day tending to the animals and the grounds, praying the entire time that he might forget about punishment he'd promised. He always remembered though. With a wicked smile on his face, he would pull me inside the barn, laughing whenever I pleaded with him to give me another chance. I would beg, promising to try harder... be better, more obedient, but he was completely unaffected. I soon learned it was pointless. He relished in the pain that he inflicted on me; I could see it in the way his eyes would glaze over. It seemed my pleas were just a pre-game warm-up filling him with anticipation for the main event. He was one sick son-of-a-bitch.

Over time I got stronger. I learned to take myself out of the moment, dreaming of the day I might be able to get away – the day I would be free from him. I was almost fifteen before that time finally came. That was the night he almost killed me. The night he decided to trade in his leather strap for a strand of barbed wire. As the metal spikes gouged into my back, he'd yank them free, ripping away my flesh. When he was done, he left me to bleed to death in one of the horse stalls. I had no idea how long I'd been lying there when Emerson managed to sneak out to help me. She tended to the wounds on my back and shoulders, crying the entire time. She pleaded with me to run away, to get away while I still could. I knew she was right. I didn't have a choice. I took the clothes and food she'd thrown in my backpack and left. I hated that I had to leave Emerson behind. I wanted to take her with me, keep her close. But I knew Grandmother Louise would look after her and keep her safe, something my grandfather would never allow her to do for me.

I thought that living on the streets would be better. I thought I'd be able to free myself from all the abuse, fear and suffering my grandfather inflicted on me, but 1 was wrong. So fucking wrong. I'd only traded one hell for another. What my grandfather failed to teach me, I learned the hard way while living out on the streets. I was scared all of the time, and starving most of the time. There was no one that I could trust; it seemed like everyone was out to get me. I had to be smarter and meaner than any of the filth that surrounded me. I stole. I fought. I even killed a guy – stabbed the son-of-a-bitch right in the throat when he tried to force himself on me.

The hunger, the fear, and the emptiness almost broke me. When I'd finally had enough, I decided to take the advice of a man who ran a halfway house down on the eastside. He was more decent than most and he seemed to really care about the kids that came to him over and over. He told me that since I had managed to stay out of jail, there was a good chance that I could join the military.

Despite how much I loathed my grandfather, I decided it was something I needed to do. Maybe it was to prove the old man wrong, show him that I could face adversity and thrive. It was probably the same reason my father joined all those years ago, just to prove that bastard wrong. Regardless of the reason, I needed the stability the military could give me. I craved it and being in the service was one of the best things I'd ever done. My troop became my family. We trained together… fought together. We became stronger, more disciplined together. It was the first time I had someone watching my back, caring whether I lived or died and I was actually happy there. I figured I'd spend my life serving my country, but just when things were going well, everything fell apart. My platoon was transporting supplies to one of the neighboring villages when the lead carrier ran over a land mine. Soon after the second carrier was ambushed, leaving most of my troop either dead or dismembered. It was a sight that will be forever burned into my memory. Seeing my brothers either dead or missing limbs broke something inside of me. The old hardness and coldness returned. Whatever weakness or compassion that was left in me was wiped out that day. When I left the service, I was capable of doing unthinkable things, and I could do them without a touch of remorse.

They say your past defines you. I'd say they were right.

Chapter 1

WREN

"FIVE MORE MINUTES, and then it's time to finish up your homework and have dinner," I warned Wyatt. He looked so content sitting at the end of the sofa with his little legs tucked underneath him. His fingers were rapidly tapping the screen as he worked diligently to create a new world on his video game. The things he could create on that little device always amazed me.

"But I'm just about to slay the dragon," he whined, never looking up from his game. His little nose crinkled into a pout at the thought of having to stop.

"Don't even start, mister. You know the rule." He'd been playing since we got home from school, and he'd keep playing all night if I let him.

"Okay. Five more minutes," he answered in defeat. His shaggy brown hair dangled in front of his eyes, making me wonder how he could even see to play his game.

"Dude. I think it's time for a haircut."

He quickly ran his fingers through his bangs, brushing them to the side and said, "No way! This is how it's supposed to look." He gave me a quick glare, his dark eyebrows furrowed in frustration before he looked back down at his game. Seeing him sitting there, I couldn't help but smile. He looked like your average eight-year-old boy with his wrinkled t-shirt and jeans, but to me, he was anything but average. I could see that Wyatt was an exceptional child, always marveling at all the wonders of the world. Every day he'd share something new he had learned, eagerly telling me every single detail of what he'd discovered. I loved hearing the excitement in his voice when he spoke, flicking his wrists at his sides as he focused on what he was saying. I had no problem admitting that my entire world was wrapped up in that little boy and there was nothing better than seeing him happy.

"How about fish sticks for dinner?" I offered.

"Nah. I want chicken nuggets."

"Wyatt, you had those last night. You're going to turn into a chicken nugget one of these days," I laughed.

"That's physically impossible, mom. Chickens are birds. People can't turn into birds," he fussed, shaking his head.

My child, always so literal. I smiled and said, "I know, buddy. I was just teasing. Are you set on chicken nuggets?"

"Yeah. I won't get them tomorrow night. Dad never has them at his house," he grumbled as he turned off his game. His brown hair fell into his face, hiding his look of disappointment. I cringed at the thought of him going to his dad's. He'd been going to his dad's every other Thursday for months, but it was still hard for him to transition from one house to the other. It also didn't help that I was terrified every time he had to go stay with his dad. I tried my best to hide my concerns from him, but I could tell that he sensed something was wrong.

I started dating his father, Michael, when we were still in high school, and I absolutely adored him. I loved that he was so strong and protective, not to mention devastatingly handsome. He came from a good home and was extremely close to his parents which I loved...at the time. I felt safe wrapped up in his arms, thinking that our love for each other would be enough to see us through anything. Back then, I really thought we'd spend the rest of our lives together. Unfortunately, the thing that I loved the most about him ended up being the very thing that scared me the most about him. Over time he became controlling and jealous to the point that I felt suffocated by him. I was nearly paralyzed by my inability to make a move without his approval. If I didn't do things the way he expected me to, he'd get angry, so very angry. His temper was a force to be reckoned with. When he snapped, I didn't know how to protect myself from his wrath. I'd tried everything from talking him down with reason to silently enduring it. Nothing worked. I'd known about the fights he'd had at bars and various other places when his temper got out of hand, but I never thought that he'd be like that with me. The first time I saw the flash of rage that crossed his face was directed at me, I was stunned. I wasn't expecting him to be thrilled that I had gotten pregnant so early in our marriage, but his intense anger caught me completely off guard. I'll never forget the way he looked at me when he reared back his closed fist and slammed it into the side of my head. It was like he wasn't even the same person. That beating was so bad the doctor was surprised that I didn't miscarry.

Michael cried for days afterwards, pleading with me to forgive him. He promised—he swore to me—that it would never happen again. Michael said he would do whatever it took to make our baby happy. I hadn't even finished college yet. If I left him, I would end up moving in with my parents and raising my child without a father. Truthfully, I loved my husband, and I wanted –

no, I needed – to believe him. I had to trust him when he said he would take care of us and give us the life he'd promised. Even though I was only a few months pregnant, my child had already become the most important thing in the world to me. It's one of the reasons I named my son Wyatt, my little warrior. At the time, I had no idea how much the meaning of that name truly suited him.

In reflection, I should've left Michael that night and never looked back. I honestly thought the incident would be a one time thing. I told myself that the shock and stress from the news of my unexpected pregnancy had just completely overwhelmed him and caused him to totally flip out. Unfortunately, I couldn't have been more wrong. The attacks were sporadic but effective. I never knew what was going to set him off, and over time, I became a different person. I hated that I didn't stand up for myself more, demand that he treat me better, but the fear was just so all consuming. I eventually learned to do whatever I could to make him happy, always trying my best to keep the peace. I was finally learning to deal with Michael and his temper, but when we found out about Wyatt, things got worse.

As Wyatt got a little older, I became worried that he wasn't talking like most of the children his age. When I finally took him to be tested, they informed us that he had Asperger's Syndrome, a form of autism that causes some children to have trouble with social interactions, and they often exhibit a restricted range of interests and repetitive behaviors. It was a heartbreaking discovery, but I still managed to remain hopeful. Wyatt was a wonderful little boy, and I loved him just the way he was. Unfortunately, Michael hated that his son was different. Image was everything to Michael. He was fixated on us appearing as the perfect all-American family, especially to his parents, and he blamed me for Wyatt's delays. Ultimately, I ended up in the hospital for five days with three cracked ribs, a broken wrist and slight head trauma, all due to his frustration with our son. That night changed everything. I was done trying to make things work with an abusive husband. I gathered up all the courage I could muster, and I pressed charges against him. It's one of the reasons he now has supervised visitation with Wyatt and had to attend anger management classes for a year. The classes seemed to be helping him, but they didn't make me feel any better about sending Wyatt over there. I just don't trust Michael, but in the end, the courts left me no choice.

When Wyatt caught me staring at him, he asked, "So, are you going to make nuggets?"

"Yeah, I'll make chicken nuggets, but you're going to have to eat some vegetables, too," I told him as I headed towards the kitchen.

Wyatt reached for his backpack and followed me, tossing his things on the floor by the table. "Okay, but no broccoli. I hate broccoli. And I got a one hundred on my math test today," he told me, pulling his books out and placing them on the kitchen table.

"That's great, buddy, but I'm not surprised. You always do well in math."

"It's my favorite," he confessed.

"I know. It was always mine, too. Since you did so well, you can have a few extra minutes on your game after dinner."

As usual, I got no response. He knew he earned extra time on his game when he made good grades, so after dinner, he curled up in his favorite spot and finished creating his new world. When he was done, he headed for the shower without being told. I searched through his drawers looking for his favorite pajamas and laid them on his dresser. I sat down on the edge of his bed and waited for him to finish up in the bathroom. The shower turned off and seconds later I heard Wyatt's wet little feet slap against the hardwood floor as he headed down the hall. He stopped at the doorway and stared at me with one towel wrapped around his waist and another around his head.

"What's up, Buddy?" I asked.

"Nothing," he answered as he walked over to me and wrapped his little wet arms around my neck. When I wrapped my arms around him a mix of fruity shampoo and my favorite body wash surrounded me. I held him tight against my chest, kissing him lightly on the side of his head. I cherished those moments. Wyatt isn't one to give affection often, but when he does, there's no better feeling in the entire world. There was a time when he wouldn't even talk to me much less touch me, so I held him close, enjoying the moment while it lasted.

"Time for bed, momma," he told me, pulling free from my embrace. He reached for his clothes and started to get dressed, letting me know that he didn't need my help.

"I'll be back in a few minutes to check on you," I told him as I got up and started to leave. "Love you, Buddy."

"You too," he replied while he crawled into the bed. I went back to check on him fifteen minutes later, and he was already sound asleep.

The next morning Wyatt was already up and getting dressed by the time I had gotten out of the shower. When he finished getting ready, he stood at my bedroom door, sporting his favorite pair of red tennis shoes.

"Ready," he told me with a wide smile.

"Breakfast?" I asked.

"I got a granola bar."

"You know that's really just a snack, but I'll let it slide today," I said, playfully rolling my eyes at him "Want some juice or something?"

He shook his head no and headed out the front door towards the car. Overall, it was a great morning, and things continued to go well until I got to my last class of the day. I'd always wanted a career in family counseling and after my divorce, my parents encouraged me to go back to college to get my degree. They helped pay for my classes until my financial aid kicked in, and Mom helped with Wyatt when I was in class. I couldn't have done it without them, and things were going really well until I started my Counseling Theories class.

"I don't know how much more of this I can take," Rachel whined. "He has to be the most boring man on the planet."

"I feel ya, girl. I'm on my second cup of coffee, and I'm still having a hard time staying awake," I grumbled. I was just a few classes away from graduating, but first I had to survive Professor Halliburton. Thankfully, I had Rachel there to keep things interesting. I'd met her last semester in my Crisis Management and Prevention class when she asked to borrow my notes, and we'd been friends ever since.

"It's his voice. Seriously, every time he opens his mouth, it's like nails on a chalkboard," she said, drawing out her words as she spoke.

Several heads turned and looked in our direction when we both started laughing. "You're a nut, Rach."

"Hey, you want to catch a movie after the gym tonight?"

"I wish I could, but I can't. Wyatt will be with his dad after school, so I'm going to try to run some errands." I wasn't exactly lying; I really did have lots to do. My laundry was piling up, and I had to get some studying done, but those weren't the reasons I didn't want to go. I knew I wouldn't be able to enjoy myself knowing that Wyatt was with Michael.

"Wren, we both know why you don't want to go, but I get it. I know it's hard sending him over there."

"I'm sorry. I just get so anxious when he has to go over there. It's like I'm always waiting for the other shoe to drop," I explained.

"I can only imagine. It has to be just as hard for Wyatt," Rachel told me.

"It is, but at least he has Mrs. Daniels. I don't know what I'd do without her. She's really good with him."

During our divorce, Michael fought hard for joint custody of Wyatt. Sadly, it had nothing to do with being with Wyatt. No, it was just another way for him to try to hurt me, to exert his control over me. He thought he was being so clever, but I knew *exactly* what he was doing. His random calls to check in on *his son* were never about Wyatt. It was just Michael's chance to interrogate

Wyatt on what I was doing or where I'd been. Pushing for joint custody was just his vindictive way to get my child support reduced, knowing full well that less money would make it difficult for me to make it on my own. It was all just a ploy to make me miserable, and it was working. I didn't feel like I was making any progress, until I found Mrs. Daniels. The judge suggested her independent service company for Michael's supervised visitation, knowing that they had experience working with children with special needs. With Mrs. Daniels' background, she knew what to expect with Wyatt's Asperger's. He was high functioning, but dealing with all of his little quirks could still be difficult.

"He's lucky to have her. You both are," she said smiling. "I'll tell you what... why don't we hit the movies this weekend? We can take the kids with us and grab a pizza after."

"That sounds great. Wyatt loves Annalise, and he's been wanting to see that new Charlie Brown movie."

"Great! It's a plan then. Having something to look forward to might help me get through the next thirty minutes of Dr. Boring," Rachel said laughing.

After class, we both headed over to the gym for self-defense training. Rachel was a little hesitant about taking the class until she met the instructor, Brandon. Even though she spends most of the hour gawking at him, it's nice to have her there with me.

"Is it just me, or does Brandon look like Joe Manganiello?" Rachel asked as we were walking out of the gym.

"Hmmm… no. Not even close," I told her laughing.

"Yeah, well, he probably has a girlfriend anyway."

"For a guy with a girlfriend, he certainly keeps his eyes trained on you," I told her as my phone began to vibrate in my duffle bag.

"Really? He looks at me?" she asked like she didn't know what I was talking about.

"All the time," I told her, looking down at my phone. My heart dropped when I noticed that I had three missed calls from Mrs. Daniels. "Shit. Mrs. Daniels has been trying to call me." I dialed her number and prayed that she would answer.

"Wren?" Mrs. Daniels asked.

"Yes, it's me. Is everything alright?"

"I tried calling earlier, but I couldn't get through to you. I knew you had your class tonight, but no one answered the phone there either. I wouldn't have left, but I didn't have a choice when I couldn't get in touch with you," she explained.

"Left? What do you mean?" I asked, feeling the panic begin to grow in the pit of my stomach.

"My husband was taken to the hospital,

Wren. I called one of my associates, and she is on the way over to Michael's house now to see about Wyatt. Everything should be okay, but I wanted you to know what was going on."

"Wyatt's there alone with Michael?"

"Just until Anita can get there. He was fine when I left. Michael was finishing up some work on his computer, and Wyatt was playing one of his video games." She paused for just a second before she continued, "Wren, you know I wouldn't have left him unless it was an emergency."

"I completely understand. I'm on my way over there right now to make sure everything is okay," I told her. "Thanks for calling to let me know."

"Let me know if there is a problem. I will call Anita and let her know you are coming."

"Thanks," I told her as I hung up the phone. "I've got to head over to Michael's and make sure Wyatt's okay!"

"Why? What's going on?"

"Mrs. Daniels had an emergency and had to leave," my voice trembled. I fought back my tears as I started walking towards my car.

Following close behind me, Rachel asked, "Don't you want me to go with you? You don't need to be driving when you're upset like this."

"No. I'll be fine. I just need to get over there," I explained as I got in my car and started the engine. I didn't have time to explain why having her there would only make it harder. Michael wouldn't be happy about me showing up there early and having someone with me would only make it worse.

My mind raced with a million awful thoughts as I pressed my foot against the accelerator. I couldn't stop thinking that something terrible had happened. I needed to pull it together. Wyatt didn't need to see me upset. I took a deep breath, trying to push back the agonizing panic that was spreading through my chest. I hated it. What if Wyatt had one of his meltdowns when Ms. Daniels left? What if Michael lost his temper and hurt him? Damn. I was so sick of worrying all the time. Sick of being scared.

It was just starting to get dark when I pulled up in Michael's driveway. Looking at Michael's house, I found it hard to believe that I once called it home. Michael's parents bought it for us as a wedding present. They wanted us to have the perfect place to start our new lives together, and I fell in love with it the moment I saw it. It didn't take us long to make the place ours, and I actually loved living there. That was a long time ago. Now, it seemed so unfamiliar, haunting. The porch light was on, revealing all the leaves and dirt scattered by the front door. I shook my head as I thought about how hard I used to work to keep the place clean. I knocked on the door and tried to be patient as I waited for someone to answer. The door swung open, and Michael greeted me with an angry snarl on his face.

When he didn't say anything, I said, "Mrs. Daniels called, and I came to see if everything is okay with Wyatt."

"Of course you did," he growled.

"Look, I don't want to get into an argument with you about this. Just go tell Wyatt I'm here to get him."

He stood in the doorway, arms crossed with a smug look on his face and said, "Can't do that."

"And why's that?" I asked, trying to hold back my anger. It was so hard for me not to cuss at him. A million profanities were sitting at the tip of my tongue, but I kept them to myself, knowing I needed to keep my cool.

"He's not here," he said with his eyebrow raised in defiance.

"What do you mean he's not here? Ms. Daniels called ten minutes ago and said she left him here with you." He repulsed me. I couldn't believe that the man standing in front of me was someone that I'd actually cared about, that I had once *loved*. Looking at him now made my skin crawl.

"The little shit ran off. Just like always, he can't take it when someone tells him no. If you stopped…" Anger surged through me, and I wanted to strangle him for not giving a shit that our son had disappeared. He should be worried, scared out of his mind, but he hadn't even tried to go and find him.

"Damn it, Michael! Your eight-year-old son ran away, and you didn't even go look for him?" I shouted, turning to head back for my car. "You're unbelievable!" As soon as I got in my car, I started up the engine and headed to our secret spot, praying that Wyatt was there and that he was okay.

Chapter 2

STITCH

A TWISTED FEELING of satisfaction washed over me as I watched Victor's last breath of air seep from his lungs. I released the chain restraints that held him dangling from the ceiling, and his lifeless body plunged to the floor. I looked down at the bloody pile that rested at my feet. There wasn't much left of the man Cotton had brought in a day ago, just mangled flesh and broken bones. I had to give him credit though; he fought harder and lasted longer than most. As the Sergeant of Arms of the King Python's Syndicate, he'd tried to do what he could to protect his club, but in the end, there was nothing he could do to help them. His fate was sealed the night he put a bullet in my brother; there was no way I'd let him walk away after that. He knew I wouldn't stop until the deed was done, knowing I had every intention of avenging my brother's death. In the process, I did what I had to do to find out everything that motherfucker knew about his club trying to take over our territory. I spent thirty-six hours extracting every bit of information I could get on the Pythons. When I pulled out the blowtorch, that asshole started singing like a canary. In no time, I had everything Cotton would need to know to bury these motherfuckers.

I left what remained of Victor Gomez laying on the floor and headed out to my bike, feeling relieved to finally get out of that room. The brothers called it my playroom, and even though there were times I enjoyed dishing out my revenge, today I was ready to get the hell out of there. I'd been at it for hours, and I needed a hot shower and food in my stomach. The door slammed behind me as I headed out towards my bike. Before I started the engine, I pulled out my phone and called Cotton.

"Yeah?" he answered.

"It's done."

"Good. I'll send the clean-up over," he said.

"I'm heading out."

"Need to discuss what you found out," Cotton demanded.

"Sure thing Prez, but I need to shower and get some food in me first," I answered.

"Understood, but hurry every chance you get." I knew he was eager to hear what I'd found out, but I was relieved that he didn't push.

"Will do." I told him as I hung up my phone and shoved it in my back pocket.

My place was on the backside of town, a rustic log cabin out by the water and away from all the bullshit. I liked to keep to myself. I avoided the outside world whenever possible and the secluded cabin suited me perfectly. No one was around to ask questions, and with the life I lived, I needed it like that. As soon as I got home, I went straight to the back of the cabin. I stripped my blood soaked shirt and jeans off, and threw them into the fire pit. Then, I lit a match and watched the evidence burn to nothing. As soon as I got inside, I went straight to the bathroom and jumped in the shower, letting the steaming hot water run down over my aching muscles. I dropped my head and watched the blood stained water swirl around my feet, eventually disappearing down the drain. After several minutes, the water finally began to run clear. I grabbed my scrub brush and set to work on the muck under my fingernails. My hands were almost rubbed raw before I felt that they were clean enough to move on to the rest of my body. I pressed the brush firmly against my skin, forcing it back and forth over the scars that crisscross my back, making the bristles scratch against my flesh. Never feeling like I could wash away the filth, my shower routines had become methodical over the past decade. It was just one of the idiosyncrasies

I'd developed over the years.

The steaming water trailed over the back of my neck, and the tension in my muscles slowly began to diminish. I cupped my hands in front of me, watching the water pool in my palms, thinking back over all the shit that had happened in my life. There was a time that I didn't think I'd make it, and the only thing that kept me going was Emerson. I thought about her every day wondering if she was okay. I still vividly remember the last time I got to see her in her teens. I'd been out on the streets for over a year and didn't have a dime to my name. Out of desperation, I went to one of the local churches and swiped forty dollars out of the offering plate – just enough money to take the bus back to Mount Vernon to check on her.

When I got there, I spotted her on the front lawn of the schoolyard, talking with a couple of her friends. It was a relief to see that she looked happy. She was laughing about something, but stopped the minute she spotted me. Without hesitation, she raced over to me and jumped in my arms, hugging me tightly.

"You're here! You're really here!" she squealed.

"I would've come sooner, but…"

"I'm just glad you're here. I was so worried about you," she cried, squeezing her arms around my waist. I pulled back and stared at her for a minute. I couldn't believe how much she'd grown. She was almost fourteen

now and looking at her reminded me so much of my mother. She had the same long brown hair and crooked grin. My eyes roamed over her, searching for any signs of bruises or welts.

Emerson shook her head and said, "I'm fine, Griff. He's still mean as ever, but he doesn't hurt me."

"You know, I'll kill him if he ever lays a hand on you. Never doubt that."

"He won't. Don't worry," she told me. "Are you okay? What are you doing with yourself these days? Where are you living?"

I didn't have the heart to tell her that I'd been spending my days at the YMCA and nights in the local homeless shelters, so I told her, "I made some friends. I'm staying with them 'till I can get a place of my own."

"Good. I hated that you had to stay in those awful shelters by yourself." A tear trickled down her cheek as she said, "I miss you so much, but I'm glad you got away."

"I'm going to be gone for a while, so I won't be able to get back here to check on you," I explained.

"Where are you going?" she asked, panic filling her eyes.

"Gonna enlist. Just long enough to get on my feet… then I'll be back." I'd just turned eighteen, so I thought it made sense to join. When I'd gone in to enlist, I found out it wasn't as simple as just signing my name on the dotted line. I had to give my background, where I'd been living for the past ten years, and that was just the beginning. I was lucky that the recruiter was willing to help me. I

figured it had something to do with my last name. It was a small town, and I had no doubt that he knew my grandfather. I didn't care why he helped me, I was just glad that he did. The recruiter helped me get my GED, and I just had to pass the AVSAB next week to have everything I needed to join.

"But why? What if something happens to you?" she pleaded.

"Made it this far, Em. This is something I have to do. I'll be fine," I explained. "You better get going. Don't want you to miss your ride."

"Please be careful, and come back," she whispered as a small tear trickled down her cheek. She reached up and hugged me once more before she turned and ran for her bus. "Love you, Griff," she called back.

I got out of the shower trying to remember the last time I'd been to see her. During my stint in the service, she'd become a typical teenager, busy with her friends and dating. After she graduated high school, she started college, by then I was a full-patch member of the club. I missed the sense of brotherhood I'd found in the military and joining Satan's Fury gave me the family I'd never really had. My club and my brothers meant everything to me, and they kept me very busy. I hadn't actually seen Emerson in months, but as soon as things settled down, I planned to go see her.

It was getting late, and I was starving. Before

heading over to Cotton's office, I stopped off at a local diner for a decent meal. The place was small, a little mom and pop joint that'd been there forever. The food was good, and the waitresses let me be. They quickly figured out that I wasn't there for the small talk and left me to eat in peace. I pulled into the nearly empty parking lot and parked my bike at the edge of the lot. Just as I was about to kill the engine, I noticed a little pair of red tennis shoes sticking out from the side of the building. I used the tip of my boot to adjust my kickstand, edging my headlight over to the small shadow wrapped in darkness. A young boy, probably around seven or eight, sat with his back against the side of the building and his little arms wrapped around his knees. For a split second, I considered going inside, leaving the kid to deal with his own shit but I just couldn't do it. I couldn't leave him out here all alone in the dark.

I turned off the engine and walked over to him and instantly felt a pang of guilt when I saw the terrified look on the boy's face. "You alright, kid?" I asked.

He didn't answer, just stared at me like I was the Grim Reaper. Can't say I blame him. My size could be considered threatening to just about anyone, and my beard and tattoos didn't exactly make things any better for a freaked-out kid on the east side of town. He held his knees close to his chest as he looked up at me, trying to determine whether or not I was truly a threat. I didn't want to scare the kid, but I couldn't just leave him out here alone. Not really knowing what else to do, I shoved my hands in my pockets and leaned my back up against the wall next to him. I waited silently, hoping that he would figure out that I wasn't there to hurt him, that he might tell me what the hell was going on.

The kid remained painfully silent as I stood there next to him. I kept thinking that he might say something, acknowledge my presence in some way, but nothing. Even with the chill of the night setting in, he didn't budge from his spot. It was almost half an hour later before a car pulled out of the lot, its headlights shining down on the boy's body, revealing several large bruises developing on both of his arms. From the looks of him, someone had just manhandled the hell outta him. The sight of those bruises triggered a flood of memories from my childhood, and I was instantly overcome with fury. He was so small, defenseless, and some motherfucker... I took a deep, cleansing breath and tried to calm the rage that was building inside of me. I needed to get him inside, try to find out what the hell was going on, to see if there was something I could do to help.

"Look, kid. I'm starving," I said low and calm. "How about we go inside, and I'll buy you a cheeseburger."

He looked up at me, and I could see the wheels turning inside his head, and for a second, I almost thought he was going to agree to go inside with me. I let out a deep sigh when he started to shake his head no.

"They make really great burgers, kid. You sure you don't want one?" I tried again.

"I like chicken nuggets," he said, looking down at his shoes.

"They've got chicken nuggets."

"Okay," he said as he slowly began to stand. He brushed the dust off of his backside and started walking towards the door.

Without saying a word, he headed to the back of the diner and sat down in one of the corner booths. He rested his elbows on the table, propping his chin in his hands, and watched me sit down. As I settled in the booth, I swallowed hard, pushing back the memories of my past when I looked down at the large bruises forming on his arms. Someone was handling him roughly, and they'd done it very recently. The question was who.

After ordering our food, I asked him, "You live around here?"

"No," he answered as he played with the paper from his straw. He folded it into several different shapes, before he started arranging all the items from the table into one long line. I watched with curiosity as he methodically brought each item in and out of line until it was all perfectly symmetrical. I couldn't help but wonder what the hell was that all about.

He looked up at me, studying me for a moment before he said, "You've got a bushy beard and lots of tattoos."

"Yeah, I do."

"The internet says that tattoos are a form of self-expression. That each tattoo has an important meaning," he explained.

"I'd say that's about right."

"You also drive a Harley Davidson motorcycle."

"You're pretty observant, kid."

"Harley Davidson Motorcycles were founded in 1903, and they were first used by police officers in Detroit, Michigan," he said just before taking another bite of his chicken nugget.

I didn't know what to make of the kid. There was obviously something different about him... but I liked it. I liked *him*. When he didn't continue on with his lesson, I asked, "You gonna tell me why you're hiding out in the parking lot?"

"Momma told me to come here, to the Old Mill Café, if something bad ever happened. It's our secret place," he answered. I felt hopeful that the kid actually had a family, but I still wasn't sure who had put their hands on him.

I wanted to know exactly what *bad* thing had

just happened to him, and I was about to ask him why they even needed a secret place, when the waitress brought over the sundae he'd ordered. The minute she sat it down in front of him, he grabbed his spoon and started to dig in. He was obviously still hungry, so I decided to let him eat without grilling him for more information. It was hard for me to hold back. Finding out information was my job. And I wanted to help him, but I knew I needed to be careful with how I questioned him, seeing that he obviously wasn't like any other kid I'd ever met. I looked around the room. The diner was quiet, just an elderly couple sitting at one of the front tables. From time to time, the old lady would turn and sneak a peek at us, clearly curious about what was going on with me and the kid sitting across from me. I couldn't blame her. I felt the same way.

"Thank you," he said with his mouth full. He took a sip from his soda before he continued, "This is good."

"You got a name?"

"It's Wyatt."

"My name's Stitch," I told him.

"Your momma named you Stitch?" he asked with a confused look on his face.

"Nah. My mother named me Griffin, but all my brothers in my club call me Stitch," I clarified.

He was silent for a minute, and I could tell

that something was bugging him. Eventually he said, "My momma had to get stitches one time." He looked out the window, and I could see the worry in his eyes when he mentioned her.

"You think we should call her? Tell her you're at the special spot?" I asked.

"Yeah."

I was reaching in my back pocket for my phone when a commotion at the front door caught my attention. A young woman rushed over to one of the waitresses and started talking hysterically. Her cheeks flushed red with alarm as she spoke, and after a few seconds, she turned and looked in our direction. Frozen in her stance, her dark brown eyes slowly met mine, a stunned look crossing her face as her eyes roamed over me. I noticed that she had a lot of the same features as Wyatt, even the same freckles along the bridge of her nose. There was no doubt that she was Wyatt's mother. She obviously had no idea what to make of me, and the fact that I was sitting with her son clearly scared the shit out of her. Her troubled eyes locked on mine as she started advancing towards our booth. Wearing an oversized t-shirt and sweats, she wasn't like the girls at the club. There was a wholesomeness about her, a goodness that I wasn't accustomed to. She stopped at the edge of the table, shooting me a nervous glance, and knelt down next to her son.

"Hey, Buddy. Are you okay?" she asked in almost a whisper.

I knew instantly by the way he looked at her that she wasn't the one who had put those bruises on his arms. "Hey, Momma. This is Griffin. He got me some chicken nuggets, but I'm done now. Can we go home?"

"Hi, I'm Wren," she said, before turning back to her son. "Yeah, buddy. We can go. You did a good job getting here like we talked about. I'm so proud of you," she answered.

"Went down Tucker Street, and turned right on Main. Just like you showed me."

"You are such a smart boy," she said, brushing his long bangs out of his eyes. She looked over to me with a pleading look and said, "I know this looks bad... really bad, but I'm doing the best I can." I had no idea why it even mattered to her what I thought, but I could see that it was important that I understood. "I'd tell you what this was all about, but it would take a lifetime to explain. Right now, I need to get him home. How much do I owe you for the food?"

"Don't worry about it. I got it," I told her.

"Thank you so much," she said.

Before I had a chance to say anything else, she took Wyatt by the hand and helped him out of the booth. I stood up along with him and watched as she started towards the door. When we got to the exit, she turned towards me and reached out to shake my hand. Her touch was soft and gentle as she said, "I don't know how to thank you for this. I just..."

"Not a problem. I understand." The second she released my hand, I felt the loss of her warmth. I couldn't remember a time when someone's touch had affected me like that, and I didn't know what to make of my reaction. I just knew I didn't want her leave, not until I knew what was going on. Knowing it wasn't any of my fucking business, I stood frozen in my spot as I watched them both walk out to her car. I should've left things alone – let them walk out that door and never think about it again. But I found that I just couldn't and that surprised me.

Chapter 3

WREN

WYATT WAS QUIET as he got in the car. His little hand reached up for his seatbelt, and my heart practically shattered on the spot when I noticed the bruising on his little arms. I had no doubt how they'd gotten there, realizing instantly that my worst nightmare had come true. I'd prayed that this night would never come, but deep down, I always knew it would. I had to fight back the tears when I looked over to his precious little face. It killed me to think that his father had hurt him, and everything in me wanted to take Wyatt and run – get as far away from Michael as I could. I had to make sure it never happened again. Wyatt was such a wonderful little boy. He filled my life with so many blessings, and I just couldn't understand how Michael could hurt him. My mind was full of questions. I desperately wanted to grill Wyatt about what had happened, but I knew I needed to tread very carefully. If he

L WILDER

thought I was upset he would shut down, and I'd never find out exactly what happened.

I started the engine and said, "I'm sorry that Mrs. Daniels had to leave you tonight, Bud."

"It's okay. She had a family emergency," he answered, looking towards the diner. Something had momentarily caught his attention, causing him to turn back in his seat to get a closer look. A few seconds passed, and then he turned back to me and said, "I think it was something bad. She was crying."

"Yeah. She wouldn't have left you unless it was really important. As soon as she called me, I came for you. I'm really sorry it took me so long."

"It was okay. I knew you'd come," he said with confidence, assuring me that he knew I wouldn't let him down. The kid never ceased to amaze me. Even when everything went to hell in a handbasket, he could still see the positive side of things.

I slowly pulled out onto the highway and headed towards home. My chest ached with worry, so I took another deep breath, trying to settle my nerves. I watched Wyatt start to fiddle with the zipper of his jacket, seemingly unfazed by whatever happened. I hated to bring it all back up for him, but I needed to know what happened to him at Michael's house tonight. Taking another deep breath, I tried my best to steady my voice as I asked him, "Can you tell me what happened at your Dad's tonight, Bud?"

He looked away from me, peering out the window, and with very little emotion he said, "He got mad, so I left." His little shoulders dropped in defeat as he thought back over what had happened. I hated seeing him look so un-happy. I just wanted to reach over and hold him, hug away the hurt that he was feeling, but we were still several miles from home.

"Why did he get mad?" I prodded.

He shrugged his shoulders and answered, "I don't know. He was talking on his phone with grandma and then he started saying all these really bad words. When he hung up, he threw his phone on the table and started yelling at me."

"What was he saying to you?"

"I can't remember," he lied. He always re-membered everything – every little detail, every single word of every conversation. I knew he remembered exactly what his father had said. I just didn't know why he wouldn't tell me.

"Is that why you left?" I questioned.

"Yeah. You told me to leave if anything bad happened."

"You're right. I did." I gently squeezed his hand and said, "You did the right thing. I'm so very proud of you."

He looked over to me and asked, "Can I play my game when I get home?"

"Yeah, you can play, but just for a little while. You'll need to take a shower before bed." And just like that, he was done talking. There was so much more that I wanted to know, like how he got those bruises, but I decided not to push it further right now. He'd been through enough tonight.

As soon as I parked the car in the driveway, I turned to him and asked, "Can Momma get a hug?"

Without answering, he reached over, slipped his arms around my neck and squeezed. "Love you, Momma."

Still holding him tight, I said, "Wyatt… you have bruises on your arms."

Looking down at the bruises, he pulled away from our embrace and said, "It's not that bad, Momma."

"I'm a little worried about it. Can I take a picture of them? I just want to make sure it doesn't get any worse," I asked, as I reached into my purse and pulled out my phone.

"Okay," he answered, holding out his arms for me. As soon as I took a couple of pictures, he jumped out of the car and ran towards the front door. I looked down at my phone to make sure the pictures were clear, knowing I'd need the evidence if I wanted to keep Michael away from Wyatt. Once we were inside, Wyatt spent a half an hour playing his game, then he informed me that it was time for his shower. After I got him situated, I decided to call Mrs. Daniels. I wanted to see how her husband was doing and let her know what had happened with Michael.

"Hello?" she answered.

"Hi. It's Wren. I just wanted to call and see how your husband was doing."

"He's going to be fine, dear. He had one of his spells with his blood sugar, but they were able to stabilize him."

"I'm glad he's going to be okay. Do the doctors know why it happened?"

"His diet. The man is so damn stubborn. I've been telling him to watch what he's been eating for weeks, but he just wouldn't listen to me. Always sneaking little treats behind my back. Now, he won't have a choice," she explained.

"Well, hopefully he learned his lesson today," I said teasingly.

"Doubt it. He'll never learn," she laughed. "I'm just sorry that I had to leave Wyatt like I did. I was just getting ready to call you. Was everything okay with Wyatt when you got there?"

"*No...* it wasn't. I'm still not exactly sure what happened, but Wyatt ended up running away from Michael's house."

"What do you mean he ran away?" she shrilled.

"Something happened with Michael. I can't get Wyatt to tell me what happened, but it was bad enough to make him run away. I found him at the diner a few blocks away from Michael's house. He seemed okay, but he has some pretty big bruises on his arm," I told her.

"What kind of bruises?" she asked.

"It looks like Michael may have grabbed him, but I'm only guessing. I hate that he won't tell me what happened."

"Wyatt's a smart boy. I'm sure he's just scared, but he'll talk about it when he's ready. Just give it a little time," she said, trying to reassure me.

"It's just so hard. I feel so guilty... like this whole thing is all my fault," I started. After wiping the tears from my eyes, I continued, "I'm his mother! It's my job to protect him from things like this," I sobbed.

"Don't do this to yourself, Wren. None of this is your fault. It's an awful situation, but you've managed to make the best of it."

"I just hate that Wyatt has to go over there at all. I've got to do something."

"One thing at a time, Wren. First, you've got to get Wyatt to talk about what happened there tonight."

"I'm not sure how to do that. He tends to keep everything bottled up inside, especially when he thinks it's something that will upset me."

"Is there someone else he could talk to?

Someone that he trusts?" she questioned.

"He might talk to Jenny, his behavioral therapist. She's been amazing with him. She's the only person I can think of that might be able to get him to open up. I'll tell her what happened and see what she can do."

"Good, I think that's a great idea. I'll go into the office tomorrow and file an incident report on what happened tonight. The judge won't be happy about this at all. Hopefully, we can get the visitation suspended or, at the very least, reduced," she explained.

"And I took pictures in case you need them."

"Good. Absolutely, send them to me as soon as you can."

"I'll do it now. Thank you for everything. You've been a godsend to me and to Wyatt."

"Oh, Wren... try not to worry, OK? You're a wonderful mother, and Wyatt's so lucky to have you as his mom."

Just as I was hanging up the phone, Wyatt darted out of the bathroom, running across the hall as he held a towel around his waist. Once he made it to his bedroom, I gave him a few minutes to get dressed before I went to his room to tuck him in. He was already under the covers when I walked in.

"Did you brush your teeth?" I asked.

"Yep, and I hung up my towel," he proudly responded.

"Well, look at you being all grown up."

"When I get older, I'm going to get a Dive tattoo, and I'm gonna have a beard. A big one."

"Is that right?" I smiled. His eyes sparkled with wonder, and I knew that he was thinking about the biker from the diner. I couldn't believe after everything he'd been through tonight, he ended up at a table eating with a guy from some motorcycle gang. He was the toughest looking guy I'd ever seen, and he was looking after my child! Surprisingly enough, he didn't frighten me or Wyatt. I thought back to the moment his hand met mine, and I gently brushed the tips of my fingers over my palm, trying to hold onto the memory of his touch. There was something comforting about his presence that I didn't understand. I should've been scared that he might do something to hurt Wyatt or me, but I just didn't feel that way at all. After my experience with Michael, I'd learned what danger directed at me felt like, and I didn't get those feelings from Griffin.

"And I want a leather jacket like Griffin's."

"Yeah, his jacket was pretty cool. So how exactly did you end up meeting Griffin?" I asked curiously.

"I was waiting for you outside the diner. He saw me when he drove up, so he came over and waited with me. Then he got hungry and asked if I wanted a cheeseburger. I told him no. Then he said they had chicken nuggets," he explained.

"Chicken nuggets are your favorite." I couldn't believe that this complete stranger went out of his way to make sure Wyatt was safe. I couldn't imagine what he must have been thinking, waiting out there with such a young child at night.

"Yeah. And they were really good. We should go eat there again tomorrow night," he said with a bright smile.

"We'll definitely go back."

"Maybe Griffin will be there," he said optimistically.

"Yeah, you never know. Either way, it was really nice of him to stay there with you. I wish there was something I could do to thank him."

"You could make him one of your pecan pies like you made for the neighbor when she watered your plants."

"Maybe so," I told him, even as I knew there was very little chance of that happening. I didn't know anything about the man, and I knew it was unlikely that I would ever see him again.

"Night momma," Wyatt whispered as he turned to his side.

"Night sweetheart." I leaned over and gave him a quick kiss before heading back to my room. With my mind still racing over everything that had happened tonight, I slipped into my bed. Just as I was turning off my bedside light, I heard the sound of a motorcycle engine roar to life outside my window. I almost got up to check, but decided my mind had to be playing tricks on me.

Chapter 4

STITCH

I WAS LATE. Cotton was expecting me hours ago, but my little detour set me back. My mind should've been focused on the club and everything that I'd found out from Victor, but I couldn't get them out of my head, either of them. That worried look on Wren's face was burned into my memory, making it impossible for me to forget her. It reminded me of Emerson and my grandmother when I was being dragged to the barn.

I thought if I just followed them home and made sure they were safe, that I'd be able to let it go. Unfortunately, being there only fueled my need to know more about them. I watched them walk into that little house, half the size of my own, and I found myself wondering what they were doing inside those walls. I'm not sure what compelled me to stay as long as I did, but I couldn't leave until all the lights were off, and I knew they were safely tucked away in their beds.

When I finally made it back to the clubhouse, Cotton was drinking a beer at the bar. He spotted me coming in the front door and roared, "Where the fuck have you been?"

"Had something I needed to take care of." I had no intention of explaining where I'd been or what I'd been doing. He'd have all kinds of shit to say if he knew I'd been sitting outside some woman's house for the past hour, and I didn't want to hear it.

"From now on, take care of your shit on your own time. The club comes first, and I hate fucking waiting," he scolded.

"Let's talk in the office," he ordered as he stood up to leave. I reached into the cooler, grabbed myself a beer and followed him down the hall.

After shutting the door behind us, he went over to his desk and sat down, pulling his cigarettes out of his shirt pocket. As soon as my ass hit the seat, Cotton snapped, "Tell me."

"There's more of them holed up at one of the warehouses at Port Angeles Mill."

"How many?" he asked while lighting his cigarette.

"Three or four. Maybe more. He said they'd been gathering intel on us for weeks, could be longer," I clarified. "Everything's on some computer in the warehouse."

"Gonna need to see what they've got."

"Absolutely. Victor's disappearance is going to have ramifications, as well. They'll know something's up."

"We'll need to make a move before they have a chance to get back up. Plan to head out before daybreak. I'll call in Guardrail and Maverick."

"Won't need 'em," I clipped.

"Maybe not, but they're going with you along with a couple of the prospects," he said. Even though I knew it would be easier to go in alone, I also knew better than to try to argue that point with him.

"Ready to bring these motherfuckers down, Prez. No dicking around. They're already making plans to start distribution."

"Yeah, well… they'll have to get through the club and you first," he snickered. He was right about that. Cotton knew that I would do whatever it took to protect the club and my brothers, and I intended to do just that.

"I need some shut eye before we leave. I'll be back in a couple of hours," I told him.

When I left his office, I went straight to Big Mike's room. It was late, but I knew he'd be up. He was always working on something. Hacking, rerouting, I don't even know what the hell he does in that room, but he's a genius with a keyboard. Big Mike just had a way with computers that I couldn't even begin to understand, so I knew he'd be able to help me without drawing any unnecessary attention.

My knuckles had barely made contact with the door, when he shouted, "Yeah?"

When I opened the door, he was sitting at his computer, feverously typing away. His fingers froze as he watched me walk into the room. "Need you to do something for me."

"Whatcha got?" he asked, turning his chair from his computer to face me.

"Not much for you to go on. Just an address and two first names. I'd say the woman's in her late-twenties. She goes by Wren, and she's got a young boy that's probably seven or eight named Wyatt." I told him as I handed him the scrap of paper. "Need everything you can find on them."

"You need it now?" he asked, rubbing his red eyes.

"Next few days will do."

I didn't wait for a response as I turned to leave. I got on my bike, and even though I only had a few hours till I had to meet back up with my brothers, I took the long way home. I needed some time to clear my head. It was one of those times that I needed all my focus to be on my club. But seeing the bruises on that kid's arms brought back an onslaught of memories that I just couldn't ignore. I remembered how it felt to be afraid all the time, living in a constant state of dread and the pain. God, I'd never forget the pain. There were times when I wondered what my life would've been like if someone had been there to put a stop to it, to end the hell that I was living through, but there was no one. Nobody had ever come to my rescue.

I laid down on my sofa in an attempt to catch a few hours of sleep, but it was utterly useless. Every time I closed my eyes, they were there — my grandfather's cold, glaring eyes. The kid with the red tennis shoes, arms all bruised up and his mother's pretty but worried face. And that damn leather strap. The memories all ran together. I couldn't get away from it, so after a restless few hours of tossing and turning, I gave up and checked the clock. Seeing that it was just before dawn, I pulled myself out of bed and headed to the clubhouse. When I drove through the gate, just like Cotton had ordered, Maverick and Guardrail were waiting for me with two pro-spects. Guardrail had chosen to take Two Bit and Q' with us. He'd chosen well. Not only were they were loyal to the club, they were close to being patched in. They could be trusted, and it didn't hurt that they both could make a clean shot. We'd need them if things got heated, and it would be a good opportunity to see if they really had what it took to become a brother.

Without turning off my bike, I told them, "Let's get this thing done."

With a quick nod, they all loaded up, following me one-by-one, out to the docks. After a thirty mile drive to Angeles, we pulled up to a secluded warehouse, located just a few yards off of the main road. The lot was overgrown with weeds and cluttered with litter. The building looked deserted; it was dark and uncomfortably quiet. We dismounted from our bikes and headed towards the rear entrance. As we approached, I couldn't help but notice that the side door was bolted shut. After using my bolt cutters to remove the lock, I lifted the rolling, overhead door. I was the first one into the building, the others following right on my heels. I quickly searched the area as my brothers got into position. Two Bit stumbled across an old anchor line and slammed his shoulder into the wall, causing a loud crash to echo throughout the warehouse.

"Fuck," Maverick growled. "Get the hell back, dumbass." Embarrassment flashed over Two Bit's face as he stepped behind Guardrail.

"Gotta move," Guardrail grumbled, aiming the tip of his gun towards the back of the warehouse.

Steering the prospects into the shadows, Guardrail headed towards the rear of the building. Maverick followed as I searched for the stairs Victor had described that led up to the main office. Knowing what was on that laptop, I was determined to find it – I didn't care how long it took, what I had to do or how many motherfuckers I had to kill to get it. I wasn't leaving that fucking warehouse without it. Silence encased us as we made our way through the darkness, making my heart beat excitedly. It is what I lived for—the thrill of the hunt. Anticipation coursed through me as we headed towards the small metal staircase, causing all of my senses to sharpen and snap into high alert. We'd only taken a few steps when the hairs on the back of my neck stood tall, letting me know we weren't alone. I had no doubt that someone was watching our every move. I could feel their eyes on me, and it was only a matter of time before all hell would break loose. I looked forward to it, burned for it. Being in the heat of the battle gave me a release unlike anything I'd ever experienced before.

The old steel steps moaned with our movements, making it impossible to hide our location. We'd almost made it to the top when the office door flew open, and we were greeted with the end of a double-barreled shotgun. I didn't stop, I didn't think. Adrenaline was now pumping through my veins as my instincts took over. I reached out, grabbing the end of the gun with my hand ramming it into the guy's chest. The force of the hit threw him off balance causing him to fall back against the door, giving me the opportunity to take my shot. Seconds later, his body dropped to the ground, blood rushing from his wound. With one hard shove, I kicked him out of my way, watching the lifeless figure drop to the ground beneath the stairs.

Commotion stirred inside the office, letting me know there were more guys inside. Without stopping to seek shelter, I advanced towards the door. Maverick called out to me, trying to stop me, but my mind blocked out everything – everything except what was waiting for me on the other side of that door. As I reached into my back holster for my second gun, I struck the middle of the door with my boot, splintering it on its hinges. Gunfire instantly exploded through the room; bullets whipped past me at every angle. Without budging from my spot, I squeezed my trigger and released several rounds, instantly killing the two men that cowered down in the corner of the room. Satisfaction washed over me as I watched their dead bodies slump to the floor.

"Goddamn it, Stitch," Maverick shouted. "You're gonna get yourself killed doing shit like that."

"Still standing, ain't I?" I mocked.

"Seriously, brother. That was fucking insane," he said.

I surveyed the room and found the laptop on a small desk. I picked it up and said, "Got it."

"Thank, fuck." Maverick walked over and grabbed the laptop, then turned to me and grumbled, "Let's get the hell out of here."

When we reached the bottom of the stairs, Guardrail was waiting for us with the prospects. I turned to him and asked, "You find the fourth?"

"Two Bit got him," Guardrail announced grinning.

"Redemption," Maverick gloated. He gave him a quick slap on the back and said, "We're heading back. You and Q' get this shit cleaned up, and make it fast. You have a half an hour before daylight."

"On it," Two Bit answered as he grabbed the two gas cans.

I trusted the prospects, so I got on my bike and said, "Heading back to the club house."

Maverick and Guardrail followed me, but went their separate ways once we hit town. As soon as I got back to the clubhouse, I went straight to Big Mike's room to drop off the laptop. He was already waiting for me when I walked into his room.

"This it?" he asked as I handed him the laptop.

"One and only."

"I'll start on it now, and hey... I got something for you," he said, handing me a thick yellow envelope. "That's what I've gathered so far on the info you gave me. I'll let you know if I come across anything else."

"Thanks, brother," I told him, shoving the

envelope in the side pocket of my cut as I turned to leave.

I was still buzzing from my adrenaline high, and I needed something to settle me down. Tristen was just the girl to give me what I needed. When she'd fallen upon hard times, Cotton had given her access to one of the empty rooms until she got back on her feet. After knocking on the door, I walked in. She sat up in her bed, quickly rubbing the sleep out of her eyes. A coy smile of understanding spread across her face as she pulled the covers back and lowered herself to the floor. Her eyes sparkled with lust as she reached out to release me from my zipper. As I looked down at her, the realization that my cock wasn't even half-mast made it clear that I wasn't going to get the relief that I needed from her. The second she touched me I pulled back... Something was gnawing at me – my mind was in a cluster fuck. A daunting feeling that something big was about to go down, something that could change everything, it consumed me. I couldn't stop thinking about the safety of my brothers and that boy from the diner and his mom. I had to know what was in that folder. I backed up, looked down at Tristen. "Never mind, darlin'. Go back on back to bed and get some sleep."

Chapter 5

WREN

"I'M SO SORRY, Wren. I went over everything with the judge, but he just wouldn't listen," Mrs. Daniels explained. She'd called me right after she left the courthouse to let me know what the judge had decided about suspending Michael's visitation with Wyatt.

"So that's it?" I asked.

"No. We still have a chance to clear this up. The judge said he would make his final decision at the hearing next month," Mrs. Daniels explained.

"I just don't see how he could believe him! The judge saw the pictures, and he knows Michael's history. It doesn't make any sense for him to take his side, now," I cried. I never dreamed that things would turn out the way they had. I felt so defeated, and my heart ached as I listened to Mrs. Daniels tell me everything that happened during their meeting.

"You know better than anyone how good Michael is at turning the blame around. He's never admitted that he was at fault for anything he's done. Why would he start now?"

"The whole thing is absurd. How could he blame me, especially with those bruises on Wyatt's arm?" I snapped.

"His lawyer is really good. He twisted everything around and told the judge that Michael was trying to protect him when he grabbed Wyatt. He said that he was trying to stop him from running out the door."

"That's bullshit. Michael didn't even care that Wyatt had ran away."

"I told him all that, but his lawyer told the judge that you taught Wyatt to leave. He convinced him that you *encouraged* Wyatt to run away from him," she continued.

"I did, but it was only for emergencies. I told him only to leave if something went wrong," I explained.

"I know that, dear. It's just that Michael's trying to make it out like you've been trying to turn Wyatt against him, using his Asperger's to your advantage," she explained softly. I knew it was difficult for her to break the news to me, and she hated that she couldn't help me. "Wren, I know this is hard, but we'll get this all sorted."

"I hate him," I confessed.

"Don't blame yourself, dear. No one would."

"What now?" I asked.

"Talk to your lawyer and make sure she knows what is going on. Has Jenny made any leeway with Wyatt?"

"She's tried everything during their sessions, but he hasn't told her anything." I felt my frustration building to an all-time high as I told her, "I don't know what else to do."

"It will be several weeks before the hearing. Hopefully, she will be able to get through to him before then."

"God willing. Thank you for letting me know what happened. I appreciate all of your hard work. Please call if you hear anything else," I told her.

"You know I will. We'll get through this," she promised.

When I hung up the phone, I was tempted to call Rachel to cancel our plans to go to the movies. With everything that had happened, I wasn't in the mood for company, but Wyatt had been looking forward to going for days.

Just as I was reaching for my purse, Wyatt came to my doorway smiling and, "It's 11:11, Momma. Are we going to do this thing or what?"

"Yeah, buddy. Let's roll," I answered as I grabbed my keys. "We'll get there in time to grab some popcorn before the movie starts."

"With butter?" he asked with a pleading look.

"Yeah, with butter."

"Awesome," he answered as he bolted towards the door. "I want a soda with mine, too!"

When we got in the car, I motioned to Wyatt to fasten his seatbelt. As soon as it locked into place, Wyatt turned to me and said, "Did you know when Charles Schulz was a kid, he had a terrier named Spike? The dog understood over fifty words, and that's how he got his idea for Snoopy."

"Fifty words? That's pretty incredible," I laughed. "I'd like to have a dog like that someday."

Wyatt continued to tell me one fact after the other about the Peanut's characters, only stopping when we pulled up into the movie theater's parking lot. Rachel and Annalise, dressed in their most fashionable fall outfits, were already waiting for us at the front door. I couldn't help but smile when I noticed that they were wearing matching boots. Rachel always made the effort to look her best, even when she was just going to a kid's movie, and she made sure that her daughter did the same. They both started waving when they saw us park the car. As I turned off the engine and started to gather my things, Rachel pointed to her watch and motioned for us to hurry.

When we finally reached them, Annalise greeted Wyatt with a big smile and said, "I'm gonna get chocolate covered peanuts!" She was a year younger than Wyatt, but acted so much older. Her wavy blonde hair was twisted into a loose bun that bobbed back and forth when she spoke.

Wyatt instantly turned to me and asked, "Can I get some, too?"

"Sure, now let's get moving," I told them as I nudged Wyatt towards the ticket counter. After we got our tickets and snacks, Wyatt and Annalise raced to the theatre. They fussed back and forth until they found the perfect spot to sit. Rachel and I trailed closely behind and managed to find two seats directly behind our two little chatterboxes.

Once the kids were settled, Rachel turned to me and said, "So, what's with the look?"

"What look?" I asked, feigning my most sincere smile.

"The look that makes me wonder if I have enough money in the bank to bail you out of jail. What's going on?" Rachel asked.

There wasn't any point in trying to avoid her questions. She wouldn't let it go until I told her everything, so I confessed, "Michael managed to convince the judge that everything that happened with Wyatt the other night was just a misunderstanding."

"No way! You mean he actually believed that asshole?" Rachel whispered.

"Yeah, he did. And to top it all off, I'm worried that the judge might actually believe that I've been manipulating Wyatt by trying to turn him against Michael," I explained.

"Well, that's ridiculous. You would never do that. Besides, Wyatt is old enough now to decide that sort of thing for himself," Rachel snickered.

"I haven't had the heart to tell Wyatt that he has to go back over there this week. I'd hoped that the visitation would be suspended or something."

"Michael needs his ass kicked. Plain and simple," Rachel huffed. She turned to me, with her eyebrow perched high and said, "You know... I *know* people."

"No you don't, and as tempting as that may be, I think I'll have to pass on taking out a hit on my ex-husband," I laughed.

"Just know that you have options," Rachel giggled.

The credits were still rolling when we got up to leave, and Wyatt started to tell Annalise some of the things he'd learned about all the Peanut characters. She quickly became bored with all of his miscellaneous facts and asked to go to the restroom. When she was finished, we all headed out to the parking lot. As soon as I opened the door, Wyatt bolted towards the car. I was about to call out to him, but the words got stuck in my throat when I saw Griffin, the biker from the diner in the parking lot. Wyatt, my normally reserved child, raced over to the burly man on a motorcycle like he was a long lost friend.

The entire scene seemed surreal as I watched them start to banter back and forth like it was something they'd done a hundred times. Wyatt smiled from ear-to-ear while he stood there on his tiptoes talking to his unusual new friend. Griffin glanced over in my direction as he handed Wyatt some kind of black box, and after giving me a brief nod, he started up his engine and pulled out of the parking lot. Wyatt shoved the object in his back pocket and waved as Griffin drove out onto the main road.

Rachel leaned over to me and whispered, "What the hell was that all about?"

"I have no idea," I confessed. I honestly couldn't believe what I had just seen. A thousand questions raced through my brain as I looked at my son. His eyes were still focused on the road, watching as his biker friend disappeared into traffic.

"Was that him? The guy from the diner?" Rachel asked.

"Yeah," I responded.

"You little hooker! You didn't tell me he was hot," she snickered.

Ignoring her, I walked over to Wyatt and said, "What did he just give you?"

"I'm not supposed to say, momma. It's in the vault," he pouted.

"No, it's not. Show me," I demanded.

He reluctantly reached in his back pocket, pulling out a small black phone and handed it over to me. I scrolled through the settings, and I was shocked to see that my number and another number I didn't recognize had been added to the contacts. I couldn't decide if I was furious or thankful that Griffin had given Wyatt a phone. I had been considering getting him one myself, but I always ended up talking myself out of the idea, thinking he was too young or Michael might end up taking it from him. I was standing there, staring at the phone screen when it happened. Rage. I couldn't believe that he, a complete stranger, had the audacity to give my child a phone without my permission. "He gave you a phone! What in the world was he thinking?"

"It's in the vault, momma," Wyatt said, reaching out and trying to take the phone from my hand.

"No, Wyatt. You can't keep this," I scolded.

"What? Why? He gave it to me," Wyatt whined. I was getting frustrated, and the parking lot was getting busy with people coming and going from the movie theater. I slipped the phone into my back pocket, without another word, and I headed for the car.

Chapter 6

STITCH

'D ONLY BEEN home a couple of hours when Cotton called everyone into church. He didn't need to explain why we'd been called in, but I knew it had something to do with whatever was on that fuckin' laptop I'd dropped off earlier. When I walked into the clubhouse, I went straight down the hall and headed into church. All eyes looked towards me, and I quickly realized that I was the last one to get there. My brothers were already gathered around the table, grumbling curses under their breath. They were all anxiously waiting to see what the huge pile of folders Big Mike had was all about. I took my seat, and Prez welcomed me with a nod as he hit the gavel.

The room silenced immediately as Cotton cleared his throat and said, "Looks like our friends up North have been busy. As we expected, everyone sitting at this table has a similar file – background checks, medical records, personal history. Big Mike has folders for each of you with everything they've been able to uncover," he informed us, with a chin lift towards Mike, letting him know it was time to deliver the news. The room crackled with tension as the brothers impatiently watched Big Mike pass out the folders to all of us.

When he approached Maverick, Big Mike gave him a troubled look as he handed him the file, letting me know the information inside wouldn't be good. Maverick's eyes momentarily roamed over the letters of his name, then he eased the folder open, quickly scanning the papers inside. His calm demeanor instantly changed, his face twisting in anger as he carefully flipped through the pages; the anger literally vibrated off of him as he looked over to me, telling me without words how bad it really was. I was the last to receive my folder. Big Mike placed it on the table in front of me, stepping to the side as soon as it was delivered.

"Fuck," I grumbled under my breath as I looked at the thick folder of information. We all knew they had shit on us, that was no surprise, but the magnitude of information before me was not expected.

"It's one thing for them to come after us, trying to end our charter, but coming after our families… that's a death sentence," Cotton growled as I opened my file.

I flipped my folder open, and an all-consuming rage instantly coursed through my veins when I saw Emerson's face staring back at me. My breath quickened to a doglike pant as I sifted through the endless pictures of my sister. Every last detail of her life was in the file. They knew what she fucking drove; they had her fucking address, her class schedule – everything down to her work time sheet. The motherfuckers even had the police report of my parents' car accident and endless information on my grand-parents. I didn't bother looking at what they had on me. They knew who I was, what I could do. They had to know that I would be coming for them. I had to fight the urge to get up and leave that instant. I wanted to find and mangle each and every one of the motherfuckers who had been watching us.

"They've gone to a lot of trouble to get this much intel. They're not going to give this thing up without a fight," Cotton explained. He glanced down at his folder and ordered, "Clutch, I want you watching over Cass. Don't let her out of your sight." Cotton didn't have an Old Lady or any kin that I knew of, but he did have Cassidy. When she rolled into the club looking for a bartending job, none of us missed the way he looked at her. He'd had that same lustful eye since, and even though he'd never claimed her as his own, we all knew she was off limits to the rest of us. He never said the words, but I had no doubt that his folder included pictures of Cassidy.

"What the fuck? They even have Henley's birth certificate. What the hell were they planning to do with all this shit?" Maverick roared.

"Mike is still working on that. There's more. Turns out we aren't the only ones the Python's have been looking into," Cotton said as he tossed a stack of files on the table. "They got the same intel on all the brothers of the Forsaken Saints."

"Does Rip know?" Maverick questioned. Rip was the president of the Forsaken Saints and Lily's father. Even though we hadn't had many dealings with them, we'd always considered them to be an ally.

"Put a call into him earlier," Cotton answered. We all knew Maverick wanted to know if Lily and John Warren were included in Rip's file, but he managed to show restraint and didn't push for more information. Even though Maverick's brother, Gavin, had been declared John Warren's father, Maverick would still want to make sure he was safe.

"Doc, you need to get the med room fully stocked and prepared for anything. We need to be war ready. Stitch, have Q and Two Bit go through all the guns and ammunition with you. I want a full inventory of whatever either of you need ASAP," Guardrail ordered, pointing to the four of us.

"I stay ready, but I'll go through and make sure we've got whatever the women and children might need as well," Doc responded.

"I keep the armory war ready, just plan on Q and Two Bit being unavailable until we've cleaned and rechecked all our ammo," I responded. "I'll get you a full report and a list of anything we might need to Guardrail, as soon as possible," I assured him.

"It's going to take some time to put a plan into action, so until we do, consider everyone on high alert… eyes on the women and children at all times," Cotton ordered the table as he hit the gavel, ending the meeting.

"I'm heading out," I announced as I stood to leave. "Going to get Emerson and bringing her back here."

"I'll help Two Bit and Q with the arsenal till you're back," Maverick offered.

I gave him a quick nod as I stood up to leave. I had to get a move on it. Every minute felt like hours wasted – I had to get to my sister.

Guardrail stopped me before I left and said, "I'll have Cassidy get her a room ready."

"Thanks, brother. I'll be back in a few hours."

Even though it was just over an hour drive to Emerson's apartment, it'd been almost six months since I'd seen her. She was in her final year at the University of Washington, and she'd been busy with her classes. I didn't expect her to be happy about leaving her studies to come back to the clubhouse with me but unfortunately for her she didn't have a choice. I had to do whatever it took to keep her safe, regardless of how she felt about it.

I knocked on Emerson's door several times but got no answer. I was starting to lose my patience, so I pulled out my cell and sent her a text. Seconds later, her door flew open and Emerson lunged at me, wrapping her arms tightly around my neck. "I can't believe you're really here! I've missed you so much!"

"Missed you, too," I told her. "Need to talk to you."

She pulled back, giving me a questioning look. It was a familiar look, one that I'd become accustomed to over the years. Emerson was a worrier. Guilt over our past troubled her, making it difficult for her to believe that I really had the life I wanted. Emerson tucked her long brown hair behind her ear and said, "Something's wrong."

"Let's go inside," I told her. I followed her inside the small apartment. I glanced around, noticing how much the place suited her. It felt like a home, comfortable and inviting.

She sat down at the kitchen table, crossing

her arms as she prepared for the news, and asked, "What's going on?"

"Gonna need you to come back to Clallam with me. The club has run into some trouble and taking you back with me is the only way I know to keep you safe."

"What? I can't go anywhere right now, Griff. I'm in the middle of the semester!"

"I know, Em, and I get that your classes are important to you, but there's no other choice. You're not safe here, and I'm not leaving here without you."

"Just wait a minute. This doesn't make any sense. Why would I need to come back with you? I don't have anything to do with your club."

I reached in my pocket, pulling out several of the pictures that were included in my file and placed them on the table in front of her. She leaned forward and her eyes grew wide as she studied all the different images of her around campus. "Who took all of these?"

"Someone who knows you're important to me, so they'll try to use you to get to me. I'm not going to let that happen, so you're gonna need to stay at the clubhouse until we get this thing sorted out," I explained.

"How long is that going to take?" she huffed with defiance.

"No idea. Could be a few weeks. Could be more."

"You can't do this to me. Not now, Griffin," Emerson pleaded. "I've finally gotten away from Grandfather, and now you want me to pack my stuff and go to your motorcycle club?"

"And what are you planning to do when they come knocking at your door? Because they're coming. You can count on that, and these aren't a bunch of frat boys I'm talking about, Em. They'll kill you, but only after they've beaten and raped you."

"Stop trying to scare me!"

"Only telling you the truth."

"What about my classes?" she asked.

"We'll figure something out... online classes or something. Mike can get you set up once we get you settled. For now, I need you to go pack your shit. We're leaving in fifteen," I ordered.

"This is crazy, Griff."

"Maybe so, but it is what it is. You know you're everything to me, and I'm going to do whatever it takes to keep you safe."

She sat quietly with a scowl on her face while she mulled everything over. I knew she had a good thing going here, and it was understandable for her to be pissed. The whole thing had come as a shock to her. Hell, she'd never even been to the clubhouse before. That part of my life had always been closed off to her, and now I was demanding that she drop everything and submerse herself into my world. It wasn't exactly fair, but Emerson was a smart girl. She knew I wouldn't ask her unless there really was no other option. Without a word, she got up from the table and headed for her room. Twenty minutes later she came out of her room carrying two large duffle bags.

"Just so we are clear… I'm not happy about this, and you need to get Mr. Mike or whoever to get me setup to work on my classes online. I'm not going to get behind, just because some bozos want to cause trouble at your club."

"Understood," I told her as I took her bags.

"Are there any cute guys at this club?" she asked smiling.

"Just get in the car, Emerson," I ordered.

"You know Grandfather is going to have a shit fit if he finds out about this," she warned.

I didn't have time to worry about his bullshit, so I decided to ignore her comment and head to my bike. By the time we made it back to the clubhouse, most of the guys were gone, busy tending to their families. Emerson reluctantly followed me down the hall, obviously feeling nervous about being here. Her eyes anxiously skirted around the room as she tried to acquaint herself with her new surroundings. I was pleased to see that Guardrail had kept his promise, and Emerson's room was ready when we walked in. There wasn't much to it – just a bed, TV and a small desk in the corner, but I hoped that she wouldn't be here long. When things settled down, she could get back to school and finish her classes. After helping her get everything sorted, I headed for the door and said, "Got something I need to take care of."

"Wait! You're leaving me?" Emerson asked, her eyes wide with worry. I knew she was overwhelmed with everything, and it would take her some time to get adjusted to being at the club. But in time, she'd figure things out, and my brothers would be there to make sure she had everything she needed.

"Won't be gone long."

"Can I go with you?" she asked. "Please."

"Can you keep your mouth shut? No questions?" I asked.

"I don't know, but I'll try," she said smiling.

She wouldn't be able to stop herself, but I still agreed to let her tag along. I hadn't had much time to sort through the entire envelope of information Big Mike had given me on Wyatt and his mother, but I'd seen enough. I'd read the report on what had happened the other night when Wyatt turned up at the diner, and even with all the bruises, his dad had managed to keep his visitation. Just like I promised, I planned to be there to make sure nothing happened.

We'd been sitting outside of Michael's house for almost twenty minutes when Emerson finally asked, "So who's in the house? Is it the guys that are after you club?"

"No."

"Okay, then, what are we doing here?" she

pushed.

"I said no questions."

"Come on, Griff. You gotta give me something here. I mean, really. You've got to admit that it's kinda weird that we're just sitting out here in the dark, staring at this house like we're waiting for some bomb to go off," she fussed.

"Just keeping an eye on things," I explained.

"What things? A drug deal? A possible shoot out?" she asked, nudging me with her elbow.

"You watch too much TV."

"You are a pain in the…" she started, but clamped her mouth shut when she saw Wren's car pull into the driveway. She watched silently as Wyatt opened the front door of the house and ran over to his mother. Her face lit up when he wrapped his little arms around her waist, giving her a tight hug. My chest tightened as I watched them together, realizing how much they both cared about one another. Wren kissed her son on the top of his head and led him to the car. Neither of them acknowledged Michael standing at the front door as they pulled out of the driveway. He finally shut the door, and without missing a beat, Emerson turned to me and asked, "Are you going to tell me what that was about?"

"No," I answered as I started up my bike. How could I explain it to her, when I didn't understand it myself?

Chapter 7

WREN

I'D BEEN THREE days since I picked Wyatt up
at his dad's, and he had completely shut down.
Like a turtle crawling into his shell, Wyatt had
closed himself off from the world around him
and as time passed, he was becoming more and
more withdrawn. When I thought back to the
other night at Michael's, I couldn't stop thinking
about the look of relief on Wyatt's face when he
saw me standing in the driveway. I knew something was wrong. My little boy was scared...
utterly and completely terrified and I had no
doubt that Michael was the one who had fright-
ened him. I'd tried everything I could think of to
get Wyatt to talk to me about it, but he just
wouldn't open up. I knew it was partly because
of his Asperger's. He'd always had difficulty
talking about things that bothered him, but it was
something more than his difficulty sharing his
feelings this time. I could see it in his face... he

was trying to protect me, thinking that whatever happened might upset me. I tried to convince him that he didn't need to worry, but nothing worked. Instead of just talking to me, he'd become distant, depressed, and sad. He'd even lost interest in his video games and just sat on the sofa with his eyes glued to the TV. It broke my heart to see him hurting, and I hated that I couldn't do something more to help him. I'd racked my brain trying to figure out what Michael might have done or said, but I knew it was pointless. Unless Wyatt opened up to me, there was nothing I could do to help him.

I had ran out of ideas until I found Wyatt digging through my purse, searching for the small phone that biker had given him at the movie theater. His face lit up when he found it, smiling wide as he studied it.

"Wyatt," I reprimanded. His head quickly turned to me, fear crossing his face as he gripped the phone tightly in his hand. "We need to talk about that phone."

"Okay," he answered, looking disappointed that he'd been caught.

"Wyatt, I think it's a good idea for you to have a phone – especially when you go over to your dad's. But I don't think we should use this phone, buddy. It was a thoughtful gift, but..."

"But I like this one, Momma. It's the coolest phone *ever*," he pleaded. I looked down at the small phone and quickly realized that his pleas had nothing to do with that particular phone. It was about that biker... he wanted the phone that he had given him.

"Did your friend tell you why he gave you the phone?" I asked.

His little eyebrows furrowed when he fussed, "Mom... I told you. It's in the vault."

"Give me a hint here, buddy, or the phone is going back."

"He said I should call him if I needed help," he explained.

I wasn't surprised by Wyatt's answer. I think I'd known all along that the phone was his way of trying to help Wyatt, but he should've talked to me about it. The list of unspoken communication was adding up, and it was time for me to find out what was really going on. I didn't know what his intentions were, but I planned to find out. I decided to pay Wyatt's biker friend a visit, but there was only one problem — I had no idea how to find him. Knowing that she knew everything about Clallam County, I picked up the phone and called Rachel.

"Time for that bail money?" she chuckled.

"Ahh, no. Not quite yet, but I do have a favor to ask," I replied.

"Shoot."

"You know that biker you asked me about? I need to find him," I explained.

"What exactly are you planning to do?" she asked.

"I don't exactly know yet. I just need to know how to find him first, then I'll decide what I'm going to do from there."

"Seriously, Wren, these aren't the kind of guys you wanna mess around with," Rachel warned. "They bring badass to a whole new level."

"I can't worry about that right now, Rach. I have to talk to him, and find out why he's taken such an interest in Wyatt. Every time I turn around, he's there. I'm pretty sure I saw him at Michael's house the other night when I picked up Wyatt."

"Hold up… you mean this guy is stalking Wyatt?"

"No, I don't think it's anything like that. I think he's just trying to look out for him, but I need to know for sure. He's never said anything to me. I just know that Wyatt is crazy about this guy," I explained. "You saw how he acted when he showed up at the movies the other day. Wyatt was so excited to see him."

"Yeah, he was pretty tickled."

"I was sort of thinking… maybe this biker guy could get Wyatt to talk about everything."

"You're going to ask some stranger to talk to your son? Oh, Wren, I don't know… I don't think this is such a good idea."

"I know it sounds crazy, but think about how Wyatt looked at him, how excited he was to be talking to him. I've never seen him like that with anyone before," I explained. "Rach, I'm desperate. At this point, I'm willing to try anything. Wyatt may never open up to me and this may be my only chance to get through to him. I have no idea how this will play out, but I have to try, Rach. I have to do something. Just tell me how to find him… please. I promise to be careful," I pleaded.

Long seconds passed before she finally exhaled a heavy sigh and said, "He's a member of the Satan's Fury MC, and from the patches on his cut, it looks like your guy is one of the leaders."

"I have no idea what any of that means. Just tell me what I need to do."

"The clubhouse is just outside of town out on Highway 113. You'll have to keep an eye out for it. Trees block the entrance, and they'll have a man guarding the gate. You'll have to get past him first. If you make it that far, you shouldn't have any problem finding him," she explained. I didn't bother asking how she knew so much about these men, knowing she'd have some wild story that would only make me more nervous about going.

"I'm going to head over there now, so I'll need you to pick up Wyatt from school."

"Okay, just be sure to call me the minute you leave there," she demanded. "And please, please, *please* be careful. Promise me!"

"I will," I promised.

I tried to block out all the nagging doubts that were bombarding my brain as I followed Rachel's directions to the Satan's Fury clubhouse. The not knowing was driving me crazy. I had no idea what it was like inside a motorcycle club-house, or what these biker people were like. If I took the time to dwell on my uncertainties, I would definitely chicken out. I just had to believe that the people at that club were just like any-body else, that they wouldn't try to kill me on the spot. I was doing pretty well until I pulled up to the gate and a young heavy set man walked over to the car door. He was wearing one of those leather vests with a white patch along the side pocket that said prospect, and his arms were covered in brightly colored tattoos. He tapped the glass with the barrel of his handgun, letting me know he wanted me to roll down the win-dow. Damn. I was so screwed.

"You lost, darling?" he chuckled. He towered over my car, resting his free hand on the roof while he stuck his head in my car and looked around.

"Umm… no sir? I am looking for Griffin. I'd like to talk to him for just a minute, please?" I explained with apprehension.

"Griffin? Sorry, darling. There's no Griffin here."

"Are you sure? He has one of those leather vests like yours, and he's kind of tall with a beard."

"Yeah, you just described about half of the members of the club. I'm letting you in, but you need to leave everything in your car — no purse, no phone, no nothing. Someone will meet you at the door."

"Okay?" I answered. I eased up to the main lot, and just like he'd said, there was a man there waiting for me by the back door. He was older than the man at the gate and much more attractive — tall, muscular with beautiful green eyes. I stepped out of the car and said, "Um... hello. The man at the gate said you might be able to help me. I'm looking for a man named Griffin."

He cocked his head to the side and looked at me like he was sizing me up. After an uncomfortable moment of silence, he answered, "You mean Stitch?"

"Honestly, I have no idea. The only name I have is Griffin," I explained.

"Come on into the bar. You can wait there while I get him."

I wasn't sure what to expect when he opened the door... maybe something kinda like a strip club filled with big, scary men with guns, but it wasn't anything like that. It was just a bar. Several men were sitting at the counter, and there was an attractive woman standing behind it serving them beers. A couple of them turned and gave me a questioning look, but quickly excused my presence and went back to their conversations.

"Just grab a seat at the bar. I'll see if I can round him up."

I did as he instructed and sat down at the opposite end of the bar, hoping to avoid any confrontations. As soon as I sat down, the man called out to the lady behind the bar, "Hey, Cass. Grab the lady a drink while I go find Stitch."

"You got it, Mav," Cass answered smiling. She walked over to me and asked, "What can I get ya?"

"A water would be great," I told her.

"You look like you could use something stronger," she teased me with a smile. "You sure you don't want a beer or something?"

"Tempting, but I better stick to water."

She reached into one of the coolers and pulled out two bottles of water, placing one of them on the counter in front of me and opening the other for herself. "So, you're a friend of Stitch's?" she asked.

"Not exactly," I told her. "Honestly, I don't really know him at all. He helped me out a few weeks ago, and I haven't had a chance to thank him." When I turned my head towards the other end of the bar, I noticed several of the men looking at me. I tried to avoid their stares by taking a drink of my water, but they weren't easy to ignore.

Cass must have noticed my uneasiness, because she said, "Don't let them get to you. They're harmless."

"Easier said than done. I've never been in a club like this before," I admitted.

"Don't take this the wrong way, but I knew that the minute you walked in. The expression on your face said it all," she laughed.

"That bad, huh?" I smiled.

"Deer in headlights," she teased. "But it takes balls to come into a place like this without knowing what you're getting into."

"Either that or I'm totally insane. My name is Wren, by the way."

Just as Cass was about to respond, her attention was diverted to the side door where Maverick was walking in with Griffin. His eyebrows furrowed into an almost angry glare when he saw me sitting at the bar. I instantly began to feel nervous. The last thing I wanted to do was piss him off, but I needed some answers... and help if he was willing to give it.

Maverick stopped at the doorway and watched as Griffin approached me. "Did something happen to Wyatt?" he asked. Tension radiated off of him as he stood there waiting for me to respond. My mind went blank. I didn't know how to answer him.

"Umm... Wyatt's fine."

"Then, what are you doing here?" he questioned. I couldn't tell if he was mad that I was there, or if he was just worried. Either way, my heart couldn't stop pounding.

"I'd like to talk to you for a minute, if that's okay?"

"About?"

Damn. One word... that's all I got. Embarrassment washed over me and I couldn't stop my eyes from roaming back to the men at the end of the bar. They'd stopped talking among themselves and were now totally focused on us, a couple of them were getting a kick out of our little show. I instantly questioned coming to him for help, and the thought of being wrong about him, made me feel hopeless.

Feeling overwhelmed and scared, I stuttered, "I don't know. Maybe I'd like to know why you've found it necessary to follow my son around and give him a phone without even telling me about it."

Before I had time to register what was happening, he took a hold of my hand and pulled me out of the bar towards the parking lot. When the door slammed behind us, I started in on him again, "It's just not right. You can't just do that without asking me first, or at least having the common courtesy to tell me what the hell is going on. I don't even know you!"

His fierce expression faded when he asked, "He didn't tell you?"

"Uhhh... *No!*" I answered sarcastically. "That's why I'm here. I have no idea what the hell is going on between you two, and any time I ask Wyatt about it, he says, 'it's in the vault!'" The corners of his mouth slowly curved into a sexy grin, and the tension he was carrying in his shoulders seemed to instantly melt away.

"Your boy did good; he keeps his word," he said sounding pleased. "I told him to keep the phone in the vault... no talking about it, but I meant to his father. Not you," he explained.

"He said that he's supposed to call you if he needs help?"

"Yeah... that's why I gave him the phone."

"You didn't think that maybe you should talk to me about that first?" I asked.

"Not at the time. Wanted him to be able to reach me if he needed me and knew that giving him that phone would be the easiest way to do it. That's why I told him I was giving it to him... so I could be there... make sure nothing else happens to him or you."

"What? Why would you do that? You don't even know us! You can't make promises like that to a boy like Wyatt. He'll think you meant what you said."

"I did mean it," he clipped. "Meant every

word."

I was lost for words and stood there stunned with disbelief. I looked up at him, studying the determined look on his face, and for some strange reason, I believed him. "But why? Why are you doing all of this?"

"I've seen the police reports... your medical records. I know what your ex did to you. I know you were able to fight your way out, but you couldn't do the same for Wyatt. I can see the fear in your eyes. I know you're worried that he'll hurt him like he hurt you. I'm going to make sure that he doesn't."

There was a storm raging behind those beautiful gray eyes – a storm I could see myself being pulled into, even though part of me thought I should fight it. I stared at him in awe, realizing that I knew nothing about him, but there was something that drew me to him. Why was he so touched by Wyatt? What had happened to him to make him want to protect a little boy and his mother? I wanted to ask, but I was afraid. All I knew was I needed help, and for some inexplicable reason... I trusted him. I don't know what came over me, but I suddenly had an all-consuming need to touch him. His eyes widened with surprise when I placed my hands on his shoulders, standing high on my tiptoes, and pressed my lips against his cheek.

Chapter 8

STITCH

I'M NOT ONE to be taken by surprise – ever – but seeing Wyatt's mother sitting in my bar... that got me. I should've seen it coming. I saw the way she looked at me at that movie theatre, all wide-eyed and totally freaked out. There was no way she was going to let that shit go and that was on me. If I was going to keep my promise to Wyatt, then I'd have to remember that he had a mother that actually gave a damn about him, and she'd do whatever it took to protect him – even if that meant coming to my clubhouse to bust my balls for trying to help.

I hadn't realized just how beautiful she was, though. Maybe it was the way she looked at me... I don't know. I just knew she was a knock-out in a totally out of my league, untouchable sort of way. Her hair was pulled up away from her face, exposing the soft curves of her face, and her clothes were classy, but sexy at the same time. With her hands on her hips, she stood there staring at me with those coal black eyes, giving me hell for trailing her kid. I liked that she didn't back down from me. I couldn't think of a time that a woman had gotten to me the way she did, and I was finding it more and more difficult to ignore the strange pull I felt towards her. The woman was tough, but there was a delicate, almost fragile side to her — a side I felt an over-whelming need to protect. It'd been three days since she'd paid her little visit to the club. Three days since she pressed her beautiful full lips against my cheek, and I still couldn't stop think-ing about her.

Emerson stepped out into the hall, blocking my path to the backdoor and asked, "Where are you running off to now?"

She'd only been at the clubhouse for a couple of days, but she was already adjusting. She'd finally gotten the chance to meet Cass and Hen-ley, and she spent most of her time hanging out with them. She seemed to be getting along pretty well, but that didn't mean she was happy about how little I'd been around. Unfortunately, it couldn't be helped. When I wasn't busy handling club business, I was gone seeing about Wyatt and his mom. My time was limited and that wasn't going to change anytime soon.

"I'll be back in a couple of hours," I re-sponded without really giving her an answer.

Discussions about the club or Wyatt were off limits. Period.

"Look... I know you've got *shit* to do and all that, but I'd like to spend some time with my brother."

"I hear ya."

"So, tomorrow? Can you spare some time to hang with your sis for a little while?" she asked with more than a hint of sarcasm.

"Yeah. I can do that," I promised. "You settling in okay?"

"Yeah. It's actually pretty cool here. Everyone has been really nice, and Cassidy and Henley have been really great. I see why you love it here so much," she smiled. "I'm really happy that you have this — the club, your brothers. It's good to see you doing so well."

"You got something to keep you busy while I'm gone?" I asked her.

Emerson looked over her shoulder towards the back of the bar and smiled when she saw Henley playing that old Pac-Man arcade game. She was wearing one of her classic, old t-shirts and jeans with her hair pulled back into a pony tail, and we both smiled as we watched her body jolt from side to side as she tried to beat the game.

Laughing, Emerson shook her head and said, "Yeah, I've got some studying to do, and Henley and I are about to finish up a Pac-Man battle. I think she's kind of obsessed with it." She leaned in closer and with her hand covering her mouth, she whispered, "I beat her high score last night, and let's just say that she didn't take it very well."

"Let's go, chica!" Henley shouted. "It's your turn. Let's see if you can beat that!" Henley danced around excitedly as she waited for Emerson to take her turn.

"Give her hell," I told Emerson as she gave me a quick hug and headed over to Henley.

"You're going down, Vintage!" Emerson mocked, just before taking over the controller. It was good to see her happy here. It made it a little easier to leave her knowing that she had something to keep her occupied.

The parking lot was busy tonight. Some of the brothers were making a fire and having a few beers to let off some steam. I was just about to get on my bike when Cotton called out to me.

"Got a minute?" he asked.

"Yeah."

"It's about the warehouse," he started. "We now know that's where they wanted to set up their deliveries. They'll be looking for an alternate location, and there are several warehouses in that area for them to choose from. I want us there first."

"We'll check the area, see if we see anything suspicious, and get the surveillance set up. If they show, we'll know about it."

"I got Big Mike on it. I told him I want the best he's got," Cotton informed me. Cotton was the kind of man that wanted things done right the first time and accepted no excuses for anything less."

"You got it. Has he gotten back to you with anything?"

"He's still gathering intel on the King Pythons Syndicate and any club that they might be affiliated with," he explained. Their club has the numbers, but not the kind to pull off a hostile takeover like this."

"Yeah, they've got some help. We're going to need to pull in some resources," I suggested.

"Won't be a problem. We've got our allies for a reason. They'll back us," he assured me.

I started for my bike and said, "I'll get them going on the surveillance."

"Good. That where you're headed now?" Cotton asked, grinning at me like a fucking Cheshire cat.

"No," I answered as I got on my bike and started the engine. "I'll get back to you."

It was still early. There was no reason for me to be there, but I needed to check on them, see for myself that everything was okay. The sun had gone down, and the chill of the night bit at the back of my neck as I parked my bike at the edge of the driveway and killed the engine. Just knowing they were on the other side of those four walls made the tension I'd been carrying around all day begin to subside. Her house was just a small brick house, nothing out of the ordinary, but Wren had done her best to make the place look like a home. There were fresh mums sitting on the porch, and she had some kind of fall decoration hanging on the front door. The lights were on in the kitchen, and I could see her standing at the window. She was talking to someone, but then stopped when she noticed me sitting there. Seconds later the front door opened and Wren was walking over to me.

Her lips curled into a warm smile as she approached me and said, "Thought I might have scared you off." Her hair was up in a ponytail, and she was wearing a pair of black leggings with a sweater. Even without trying, she was gorgeous.

"I've been around."

"I'm sure you have," she laughed. "I don't know if I'll ever get used to this whole stealth protector thing you have going on, but I've decided to just take it for what it is. I mean, it's not every girl that has her very own macho motorcycle guy sitting out in their driveway, waiting to save the day. Oh, I wonder if the neighbors have spotted you. I'm surprised they haven't called me about it." I must have made her nervous, because she was rambling. Too damn cute. "So… um, I'm making spaghetti.

Would you like to come in for some?"

"No, that's not necessary," I told her.

"It's just spaghetti, Griffin. Besides, I know Wyatt would be excited to see you." I'm sure she could see that I was considering it, so she pushed a little harder. "You don't want to pass this up. I make a mean pot of spaghetti and my meatballs are homemade."

"You don't get told no very often, do you?" I poked.

"Not really. It's a character flaw of mine," she admitted.

I'd barely made it off my bike when Wyatt came barreling out of the front door and shouted, "Hey Stitch!"

"Hey there, dude. Heard your mom made spaghetti."

"Yeah, but I'm not really a fan of spaghetti," Wyatt admitted. Then he leaned in closer to me and whispered, "You should come eat some with us, then you could eat some of mine."

"I think I can help you out with that," I laughed as I followed them inside. A hint of garlic filled the air as I walked into the small kitchen and sat down. It wasn't a new place, but Wren had done a good job in making it a home. The cabinets had a fresh coat of paint, and she'd hung plaid curtains over the windows. It was nice. I watched as she walked over to the old stove and pulled out the bread, quickly placing the hot pan on the counter.

"What can I get you to drink?" Wyatt asked.

"I'll have whatever you're having."

"Mom makes me drink milk at dinner time. She says it's good for my bones. I've told her that there is calcium in my Flintstone's vitamins, but she still makes me drink it."

"Milk will be fine."

Quietly, Wren started filling the table with food while Wyatt poured me a large glass of milk. I was mesmerized watching their little dinner time routine, and I wondered if it was always like that with them. Even though it was just the two of them they were a family and I was curious how the whole thing worked. I couldn't even remember sitting down to a meal without being afraid that something would set my grandfather off. It was different with them. It was nice, really nice.

When everything was ready Wren said, "Okay, boys. Dig in."

"Looks really good, momma," Wyatt told her. Then, he cut his eyes over to me and gave me a mischievous smile. I was liking the kid more all the time.

"I saw that, Wyatt," Wren told him, nudging him playfully with her elbow.

"It's messy, Momma, and the noodles are hard to get on my fork," he complained. He placed his fork in the center of his plate and started to twirl it around, trying to gather up the noodles. When he lifted his fork, most of the noodles dropped back down to his plate. "See... it's hard."

"If you want a brownie later, then you have to eat your dinner. Up to you, bud." And with that, he took his fork and tried again... and again... and again.

We'd spent a few minutes in silence while everyone tried to eat their meal without making a huge mess, then Wyatt asked, "You know why you can't trust atoms?"

"No. Why?" I asked.

"Cause they make up everything," he answered, smiling proudly. Wren shook her head and laughed.

"We learned about atoms in science class today. Different atoms stick together to form molecules, like two hydrogen atoms and one oxygen molecule makes water," Wyatt explained.

He spent the next ten minutes telling us everything he'd learned about atoms and molecules. Eventually, he looked down at his plate and seemed surprised to see that it was clean. "Hey, Mom, can I have my brownie now?"

"Sure. Why don't you go get them and bring 'em over to the table?" As soon as he got up from the table, Wren leaned closer to me, placing her hand gently on my arm, and whispered, "This is the happiest he's been in days.

Thank you."

"He's a great kid." I was completely captivated as I watched her hand drift down my arm, stopping briefly at my wrist while she gently squeezed. I found myself longing for her next casual touch, any small gesture that let me feel the warmth of her skin against mine.

"Want a brownie?" Wyatt asked, while he placed the entire plate in front of me.

"Thanks, but I'm gonna need to take a raincheck. I've got some things to take care of," I explained.

"Okay," he said, dropping his eyes to his little red tennis shoes.

I casually stood to leave and told Wren, "Thanks for dinner. You really do make a mean pot of spaghetti."

A bright smile crossed her face when she answered, "I'm glad someone thinks so."

They both followed me to the door and waved when I pulled out of the driveway. I still had a few hours before I needed to head to the warehouse, but I needed to get out of there. I was getting too close. Felt too good to be there with them. My first instinct had been to protect them. Up until now, it had never occurred to me that maybe I needed to protect myself.

Chapter 9

WREN

IT HAD BEEN days since I'd seen Griffin It wasn't that he wasn't around. I heard the faint rumble of his motorcycle engine when he drove by our house, but he was making a point not to be seen. I didn't understand it. I thought our dinner together was really nice. I'd even caught him smiling a couple of times when he was listening to Wyatt carrying on about what he'd learned in his science class. But, for whatever reason, Griffin was avoiding us, and I didn't like it.

After our dinner together, Wyatt had actually started to improve. His routines were falling back into place, and he seemed more like himself. Just when things with Wyatt seemed to be getting better, it was time for him to go back to his dad's. It was obvious by his mood that he was dreading it. On the way to school, he stared out the window, nervously fidgeting with the zipper of his backpack. After promising him several times that I would be there exactly at eight to pick him up, he got out of the car and slowly walked inside the school building.

A nearly overwhelming feeling of dread had been weighing on me all day, and I just knew it had something to do with Wyatt. I knew something wasn't right, and it was killing me. Maybe it was mother's intuition that was gnawing at me, but I'd spent the entire day looking at the clock, biding my time until he would be back at home with me. I was momentarily distracted from my fears when I heard my cell phone ringing. I figured it was Rachel calling to see why I hadn't made it to our self-defense class but when I looked at the screen I didn't recognize the number.

"Hello?" I answered.

"Send Mrs. Daniels a message. Tell her to get Wyatt and leave... now." Stitch said urgently.

"What's going on?" I asked with panic.

"I need you to listen to me, Wren. Everything is going to be fine. Just get the message to Mrs. Daniels."

"Okay," I answered.

"I'm here, watching him, stay calm and just trust me" That's all I got and then, the phone went dead.

My fingers trembled as I typed the message to Mrs. Daniels.

Me: Take Wyatt and leave!! Please!!

Mrs. Daniels: I'm already out the door. On my way to your house.

Me: Thank goodness. See you soon.

Completely overcome with panic, tears began to stream down my face as I thought about what could have happened. My imagination ran wild, thinking about all the different times that Michael had lost his temper with me and I was terrified that he might have finally done the same thing to his son. I don't know what I would do if he hurt him. I was about to completely lose it, when a sudden realization stopped me. Griffin was there. Griffin was there with Wyatt. Just like he'd promised, he was there making sure that Wyatt was safe. An overwhelming sense of relief washed over me. All I'd ever wanted was to know that Wyatt was safe when he was with Michael, and even though I had no idea what had happened, I knew Griffin was there making sure that nothing happened to him. Finally accepting that he wouldn't let anything happen to my son helped ease my worry.

After twenty brutally long minutes, Mrs. Daniel's car finally pulled up in my driveway. I quickly opened the door and raced outside, meeting Wyatt just as he got out of her car.

"Are you okay?" I asked, trying to steady my voice as I reached out to him.

"I'm okay, Momma," he responded, as he stepped into my arms. "Daddy was being really mean and yelling, so Mrs. Daniels told me I could come home."

"I'm so sorry all that happened, but I'm really glad that she brought you home," I told him, hugging him tightly. I held him in my arms for a moment longer before I asked, "You want to go watch TV for a few minutes while I talk to Mrs. Daniels?"

"Yeah, but I've gotta do my homework first," he answered.

"You go get started and I'll come help you in a few minutes," I told him as he headed inside. The second Wyatt closed the door, I looked over to Mrs. Daniels and asked, "What the hell happened?"

"Michael was drinking, he was slurring his words and acting belligerent. When I confronted him about it, he got angry and started making threats."

"What kind of threats?"

"He was just mad that I was leaving with Wyatt. The minute that I realized that he'd been drinking, I told Wyatt to go get his things. When Michael figured out what was going on, he said that he was going to request someone new for Wyatt's supervised visitation. He started spouting off that we've become too close, and I've become biased where you and Wyatt are concerned."

"That's ridiculous!" I was so relieved that Mrs. Daniels had been there tonight. Hiring her had been the best decision I'd ever made, and I couldn't imagine losing her. Wyatt needed her to be there, especially when Michael was in one of his moods.

"It is ridiculous and I don't want you to worry about what he said."

"How am I supposed to do that? Wyatt needs you! Surely they wouldn't take you away from him... would they?" I asked with tears pooling in my eyes.

"Michael is good at twisting things around, but there is no way he can manipulate what happened tonight. He was drinking during his visitation. I'll see the judge about it first thing in the morning," she assured me. She paused briefly, then continued, "You know, I was surprised to get your text. How did you know that something was wrong?"

"Umm..." I wasn't sure what she'd think about Griffin watching over Wyatt, so I lied. "A neighbor heard Michael yelling and called me."

"Well, it's good that they are keeping an eye on things too. I better get going, dear. I need to make sure Stan took his meds. I'll let you know what happens tomorrow," she told me as she headed back to her car. I watched her pull out of the driveway before I went back inside to check on Wyatt.

He'd already finished his homework and was watching TV when I walked in. After he finished his shower, I got Wyatt settled in bed. He laid his head on the pillow and stared up at the ceiling, quickly becoming lost in his thoughts.

"You want to talk about it?" I asked him, as I pulled his blanket over him.

"I don't like Daddy very much," he finally admitted.

"I can understand that. I don't like him very much either," I told him, giving his hand a light squeeze. "I'm sorry he was mean tonight."

"He always acts mean." I knew it was a slip of the tongue by the expression on his face, but I had to push for more.

"What do you mean?"

"He's just always in a bad mood," Wyatt explained as he turned to his side and pretended to close his eyes. With that, I knew the conversation was over. Knowing it wouldn't do any good to push, I gave him a quick kiss goodnight and went to my room to get ready for bed. I was exhausted and didn't even bother doing the dishes in the sink. After changing into my pajamas, I heard the faint sound of a motorcycle engine. My heart fluttered with hope when I thought it might be Griffin. I went over to my window and peeked outside, and sure enough, his bike was parked at the end of the driveway. A smile slowly crept over my face when I saw him walking towards the house. I slipped on my silk bathrobe and rushed out of the room.

When I opened the front door, I found him waiting for me on the front porch. Under his cut, he wore a long sleeve black t-shirt that hugged him tightly across his chest showing just a hint of the defined muscles of his abdomen and a pair of faded blue jeans that hung low on his hips. My breath caught when my eyes locked on his, making it difficult to speak. I knew so little about him. He was a mystery to me, existing in a world of danger I couldn't begin to comprehend but it didn't matter. I was trapped in a spell unable to control my body's overwhelming reaction to him. I'd never known anyone like him. An intimidating strength radiated off of him making it almost impossible to imagine that there was a softer side to him, but it was there. I'd seen it, felt it, and I couldn't stop myself from being drawn to it, drawn to him.

"How's he doing?" he asked. The faint scent of his cologne drifted around me, luring me to step closer to him.

"I don't know anymore," I confessed.

"He's a smart kid. He'll be able to see through all the bullshit."

"I think he already does... he just isn't telling me about it. How did you know something was wrong?" I asked.

"Wyatt called me... told me his dad was drinking and yelling at Mrs. Daniels," he explained.

"Michael was threatening her, saying he was going to get her fired... I don't know what I'll do if we lose Mrs. Daniels. She's so good with Wyatt, and she's the only thing that makes those visitations tolerable."

"He won't lose her," he said with confidence.

"I'm not so sure. Michael keeps twisting everything around," I explained.

"He *won't* lose her. Trust me."

I had no idea how he could make a promise like that, but I believed him. I felt certain that he would do whatever it took to make sure Wyatt wouldn't lose her. The worry I'd been holding onto slowly began to diminish, and I whispered "Thank you."

He stepped closer reaching for my waist as he pulled me towards him. He held me tightly against his chest the warmth of his body surrounded me and I found myself longing for more. I slowly lifted my head from his shoulder and looked up at him, searching his face for some sign that he felt the same way. His eyes filled with lust but he hesitated. There was an agonizing silence until he brought the palm of his hand to the side of my face, gently brushing his thumb across my cheek. He slowly lowered his head, pressing his lips against mine as he kissed me tenderly. At first, his touch was soft and gentle, but it quickly changed to something more. A deep growl vibrated through his chest while his fingers tangled tightly in the back of my hair, pulling me closer as he took complete control of the kiss. His tongue brushed against mine and the world around us melted away as we got lost in each other's arms. There was no doubt that something was building between us, and my feelings for him triggered something inside of me that I didn't expect... a consuming need for more. Without warning, he pulled back, looking at me with an expression I didn't quite understand.

"Momma," Wyatt called out, and we both froze. It was like a bucket of cold water had been tossed over us while we silently listened for him to call out again.

Griffin took a step back and said, "Go see about him."

I quickly adjusted my nightgown and robe and rushed back inside the house. Wyatt was waiting for me in his bed when I walked in.

"Momma, my head hurts," he whined.

I placed the palm of my hand on his forehead, checking to see if he had any fever. "You don't feel warm. Hold on just a second and I'll get you something for your headache."

After I gave him a dose of pain reliever, I sat on the edge of his bed and waited for him to fall back to sleep. Once I was certain that he was sleeping soundly, I headed to the porch. I eased the door open and was pleased to see that Griffin was still there waiting for me. He stood there silently staring at me and I instantly felt awkward. I didn't know what to say to him.

Chapter 10

STITCH

OVER THE YEARS, I'd been with more women than I could even begin to count, but until tonight, I'd never felt so consumed by a woman. Her touch. Her mouth. Her hot little body pressed against mine. Fuck. I wasn't prepared for how good she felt in my arms, like she was meant to be there, and I didn't want to let her go. Truthfully, it scared me, scared the hell out of me. We were from two different worlds, but I wanted her more than my next breath. I hated the thought of leaving her, wanted nothing more than to take her back in my arms and show her how much I wanted her – but I'd have to wait.

She stepped back outside and when she finally looked up at me, I could see the insecurity in her eyes. She'd only been gone a few minutes but the sexual tension was higher than ever. Her hair fell softly around her shoulders and her cheeks flushed red with embarrassment—so fucking beautiful.

"Come here," I demanded.

She wavered, but then slowly started walking over to me. Wren stopped just a few inches away and said, "I'm sorry. I thought he was asleep or I would have never…"

"Come *here*," I growled. As soon as she took that last step, I dropped my hands to her waist, instantly pulling her over to me. I leaned down and pressed my lips against hers, claiming her mouth once again. With her words still echoing in my mind, I quickly pulled back and looked at her. Surprise crossed her face when I said, "First, never apologize for taking care of your kid. *Never.* Second, I've never been one for being tied down. Don't know a damn thing about relationships but this thing between you and me – it's *going to happen*, and there are things you need to know."

"You're a good man, Griffin. I know everything I need to know," she assured me.

"No, you don't. You have no idea, but you will. Get someone to take Wyatt on Friday night. I want you at the club." I told her, then kissed her one last time before heading back to my bike.

It'd been three days since I left her standing there looking like every man's wet dream. Hell, I could still taste her on my lips and it was fucking with my head. The memory of her touch was burned into my mind, fueling my need to have her in my arms again and I was more determined than ever to make her mine.

After spending several hours in church going over everything Big Mike had gathered on the Python's, the brothers were eager to let off some steam. They'd all headed to the bar for some drinks and I decided to join them for a round before I headed over to check on Wren. When I walked into the bar, I was surprised to find her sitting there with Henley and Cassidy. She was holding a half-empty beer and was laughing at something Henley had just told her. Her hair was down, curls cascading down her shoulder, and she was wearing a low-cut black sweater that showed off her perfect tits with a pair of dark jeans and black boots. My cock got hard just looking at her. She wasn't overdone and I liked that she wasn't one of those women that wore a shit ton of make-up. She was confident in her own skin and didn't need to hide behind some damn mask.

I was standing at the counter, just watching her, when Maverick came up behind me and said, "So she's back again."

"Yeah. I guess she doesn't scare off too easily," I answered.

"I can see that. After all, she's here for you," he laughed. When I didn't respond, he said, "Yeah, enough said." He motioned over to Peyton behind the bar and had her bring us both a beer. As he handed one to me, he asked, "You planning on making something out of this?"

"I am."

"Good. It's about time," Maverick smirked. He looked over to me, noticing that my focus was still on Wren and said, "Shit, you got it bad, brother."

"Never knew," I confessed.

"Yeah, it gets you when you least expect it, but when you know... you know." He took another long drink of his beer and said, "What does she know about the club?"

"Not a damn thing."

"You think she'll be able to handle it... handle what you do?"

"She'll have to," I answered, knowing that losing her wasn't an option. Before he had a chance to continue, I asked, "When will we get word on the surveillance?" I already knew Big Mike was working on it, but I felt the need to redirect the conversation. I had no intention of discussing Wren with him or anyone else for that matter.

"Anytime now. Mike's been keeping an eye on it," he answered.

Clutch stepped between us, reaching over the counter to get another beer from Peyton. After he popped the cap open, Clutch pointed the mouth of the bottle in Wren's direction and snickered, "Now that, my friends, is a hot piece of ass."

A flash of anger rushed through me and without hesitation I reached out and grabbed his wrist, splashing most of his beer on the counter. "Watch your goddamn mouth, brother."

"Whoa... Wait a minute. Did I miss something?" Clutch sputtered, taking a step back.

Maverick cleared his throat and with a mocking grin, he said, "Yeah, you did. She's with him."

"Ah, fuck man. How was I supposed to know that? I mean look at her... she's smokin' hot," Clutch explained.

"*Clutch*," I warned.

He raised his hands feigning defeat and said, "I got it."

Ignoring their shit eating grins, I left them standing there and headed over to Wren. I'd only taken a few steps when her eyes caught mine and the smile she was wearing quickly faded to a look of anticipation. I detected a spark of hunger in her eyes as she watched me walk towards her, and I liked it. Oh yeah, I liked it a whole lot.

When I approached the group, Henley quickly turned to face me and with a devilish grin asked, "Hey, Stitch. Were your ears burning?" Wren's face instantly flushed red with embarrassment, and I found myself wondering what exactly they'd been talking about.

"Henley," Cassidy warned.

"What?" Henley asked, shrugging her shoulders. "It's not like he didn't know we were talking about him."

"Hey," Wren said in barely a whisper.

I leaned in, placing my mouth in the crook of her neck and said, "You gonna tell me what you were saying about me?"

"Umm... no," she grinned.

"Yeah, we'll see about that," I told her as I slipped the beer out of her hand and took a drink.

"Hey! I've got good news," she started.

"Yeah?"

She smiled and said, "It turns out that Mrs. Daniels was able to get through to the judge. She explained everything that happened the other night and he suspended Wyatt's visitation with his dad." Her eyes sparkled with excitement as she spoke; unfortunately, I didn't feel the same. When Mike told me all about it earlier today, I was apprehensive. Yes, I wanted Wyatt to be free from his abusive father, but I knew Michael wasn't the kind of man to take a hit like that lying down. His parents weren't going to be happy about him losing his visitation with Wyatt, and with this last stunt, he'd lost the last shred of control he had over Wren. There was no doubt that he'd end up doing something stupid because of it. I wasn't going to take any chances, so I ordered Q' to keep an eye on him until Wyatt got back from Wren's parents. I was pulled from my thoughts when Wren continued, "We'll still have to go to court in a few weeks for the final judgment but for now, he doesn't have to go over there anymore."

Deciding to let her enjoy the small victory for now, I told her, "Glad to hear that." After I took another drink of her beer, I asked, "Did you get Wyatt sorted?"

"Yeah, he's with my parents for the night" she answered, not realizing that I already knew where he was. "They have a big gaming system, so he was really excited about going to stay with them."

"Hey, Stitch… you need another beer?" Cassidy asked, looking at the almost empty beer bottle in my hand.

"Yeah, make it two," I told her just before finishing off Wren's beer. I placed the empty bottle on the counter. Without warning, Emerson walked up and slipped her hand around my waist, giving me a slight hug. Wren's eyebrows furrowed with misunderstanding as she stared at Emerson's hand on my hip.

"Hey there, handsome," Emerson said. "Figured you'd be outta here by now."

"Nah… I'm gonna stick around for a bit."

"Well, it's about time. I was beginning to think you were avoiding me," she laughed.

When Cassidy placed our beers on the counter, Wren quickly picked up the bottle and began to nervously pick at the label, avoiding eye contact with me entirely.

"Want a beer?" Cassidy asked Emerson.

"Definitely." Wren snuck a glance over in our direction just as Emerson reached up and tugged at the end of my beard and said, "This thing is getting out of hand. It's time for a trim."

"Not happening."

"Listen to your little sister. No girl is going to want to curl up to that thing at night," she said, giving it one last pull.

Wren's eyes shot over to me, and she asked, "Sister?"

I was just about to answer her when Clutch interrupted, "Stitch, Cotton wants to see you in his office."

Looking over to Wren, I asked "You gonna be okay with them for a bit?"

"Sure. I'll be fine. It'll give me a chance to talk to your *sister*," she said sarcastically.

"Talk all you want, darlin'," I told her just before I placed my hands around her hips, pulling her close as I claimed her mouth. She moaned into the kiss while her hands swept across the back of my neck, tangling the tips of her fingers in my hair. The taste of the beer still clung to her lips as I deepened the kiss, and when her tongue met mine, it sent a shock straight to my cock, making it difficult to restrain my need for her. I'd never known anyone like her. With a simple touch, she had me twisted in knots, and I wanted nothing more than to stay right there in her arms. Reluctantly, I pulled back, forcing myself to release her before I lost complete control and said, "Don't let these hellions get you into any trouble while I'm gone."

"I think I can handle it," she answered playfully.

"I'm sure you can."

Chapter 11

WREN

"HOLY SMOKES! I'M gonna need a cold shower after watching that," Cassidy said laughing. "Damn. I really, really need to get laid."

I smiled, thinking I could use a cold shower myself. That kiss had my head spinning, making me almost forget about my earlier bout of jealousy. I was surprised how quickly the green eyed monster had taken ahold of me, making me act like a complete idiot. Giving a woman the evil eye for putting her hands on Griffin. I've never been a jealous person. It was totally unlike me and finding out she was his sister, only made me feel worse.

"I'm sure you can find somebody around here who will help you out with that," Henley said rolling her eyes. "You get all the action a girl needs just standing behind this counter."

"I wish…. That kiss was the most action I've

seen in weeks. It's getting to be depressing," Cassidy pouted. "The guys don't even look in my direction anymore. It's like I've grown a third eye or something."

"Don't be so dramatic, Cass. Besides, we all know there's only one of them you really care about anyway. You could give two shits about the others," Henley fussed as she took another drink of her beer.

"Yeah, well... he doesn't even acknowledge my existence anymore. I don't get it. All the guys are watching over the women, making sure they're safe and all that bullshit. Who's watching out for me? Certainly not him! His sorry ass is completely ignoring me. Hell, he won't even look at me," she replied sarcastically. I had no idea who she was talking about, but it was obvious that his lack of attention was hurting her. Quickly changing the subject, she said, "You know what? I think we need something stronger to drink. Let's do some shots!"

"I'm in," Emerson said, sitting down on the stool next to me. "I could use a few. My thesis paper just about did me in, and I'm pretty sure the professor is going to rip it to shreds since I've missed so many days of class."

"Sounds like a great excuse to get plastered. What about you, Wren? You in?" Cassidy asked.

"Sure. Why not?" I told her, knowing I could only have a couple or they'd end up scraping me up off the floor.

It was like we had our own personal bartender as Cassidy lined the shot glasses along the counter and poured us each a full shot of tequila. She reached for the salt and limes and placed them in front of us. Then, she lifted her glass and said, "Here's to the men that drive us insane. May their tattoos fade, their muscles deflate, and their balls shrivel up!"

"You're a nut, Cassidy," I laughed. "An absolute nut!" I was so glad that she'd been able to take the night off and just hang out with us tonight. She was absolutely hilarious.

We spent the next forty-five minutes laughing and drinking as they gave me a rundown of everything that goes on at the club. I had no idea that there was so much involved with being in a club like this.

"Just remember – club business is just something you don't talk about. It's the guys' way of protecting us," Cassidy explained.

"Club business? What business?" I asked.

"It's best to just stay out of it, Wren. Trust me. I learned it the hard way," Henley laughed. "Don't worry. You'll get the hang of it."

"It's pretty awesome to have so many people that are willing to be there when you need them. When you become an Old Lady, you're part of the family. They'll do anything for you and your son," Cassidy explained.

"I don't know if I'd ever be able to get used to the whole Old Lady thing," I admitted.

"If it's right, you'll think it's the best thing that ever happened to you," Henley said smiling.

"I'll take your word for it," I said laughing.

Each of them had their own wild story to tell about the club, and my cheeks were actually getting sore from laughing. I liked being here with them, and I was beginning to understand why they chose to be involved with the club. It was awesome. Even the men were nice, trying to make me feel at home with them. I was actually looking forward to coming back.

"I wanna know about you and Sti-itch," Henley slurred.

"Umm, well... I like his lips," I giggled. Leaning closer to her, I said, "And those eyes...God, I love the way that man looks at me, like he could devour my body and soul one minute, but cherish my very existence the next."

"*Oh yeah*, I don't think any of us missed that panty-melting stare he was giving you from across the bar earlier. It was... wow," Henley snickered.

"Hey! That's my brother you're talking about, hooker," Emerson grumbled as she took another shot of tequila.

"That doesn't mean he isn't hot, smartass. You should be proud," Henley told her. Quickly turning back to me, she continued her inquisition, "Wren darling, you aren't telling us anything we don't already know. We want details. We wanna know how you, *Ms. Refined and Red Wine*, ended up with our Mr. Badass?"

"I haven't figured that out yet," I explained. "He just kind of happened."

"Girl, a man like Stitch doesn't just happen," Cassidy weighed in. "He's there for a reason."

"Yeah... that's because he's a bad... *ass*. He's the freaking club Enforcer. Enough said," Henley told us, throwing her hands up in the air. "And, he's hot. You can never go wrong with that."

"I don't know what you're talking about. What's an Enforcer?" I asked.

"It's one of the positions in the club," Cassidy started. She was interrupted when Henley said, "He's like...you know... the Enforcer. He serves and protects his brothers," Henley explained, sounding more intoxicated by the minute. "Like Batman protecting Gotham City from evil."

"Batman? Really Henley?" Emerson said, shaking her head in disbelief. "Dear lord, *do not* let Griff hear you refer to him as Batman."

"What? It's a compliment. Batman is a total badass," Henley said defensively, slightly swaying from side to side as she took another shot.

"Henley, what are you twelve?" Cassidy asked, rolling her eyes. As she poured us all another round of shots, she said, "You've got to get out more, girl."

I was just about to grab my drink when Stitch walked up behind me, wrapping his arms around my waist. The warmth of his breath sent goosebumps down my spine when he whispered, "You know if you have many more of those, I'll be carrying you out of here over my shoulder."

I leaned into him, resting myself against his chest with the back of my head on his shoulder, and teased, "Is that a bad thing?"

The bristles of his beard tickled against my neck when he said, "Not at all. Looking forward to it."

"Well, that's good, because I stopped counting after the third shot," I laughed.

"She's a total lightweight," Henley chuckled, barely able to keep her eyes open. "She's only had three. I'm on number six."

"I wouldn't brag," Cassidy scolded. "Maverick is going to have your ass when he finds you like this."

"A girl can hope," Henley said wiggling her eyebrows up and down.

Emerson turned to Stitch and said, "Just so you know, I approve."

"Of?" he asked.

"Your girl Wren. She's pretty cool," Emerson said laughing. "But, Henley's right. She's a total lightweight. You probably ought to get her home."

"You ready to go, baby?" he asked me.

"Yeah, I should probably stop while I'm ahead," I confessed. Feeling a little brazen, I continued, "But, I don't want to go home yet. Umm... if it's okay, I'd kinda like to hang out with you for a little while." Even though I'd had a great time being with the girls tonight, I hadn't really had a chance to spend any time with Griffin. Knowing Wyatt was with my parents, it was one night I knew we wouldn't be interrupted and I wanted to have a chance to be alone with him.

"You could always take her out to your place," Emerson suggested with a mischievous grin.

I looked over to him, looking a little too eager, and said "I'd love to see your place."

"Done. Grab your stuff," he smiled. He took my hand and led me outside, holding me close to his side so I wouldn't stumble and fall. When we made it to the parking lot, he asked, "Where's your car?"

"Umm... it's over there," I answered, pointing to the side of the parking lot.

"Need your keys," he said as he held my arm so I wouldn't lose my balance.

I fumbled around in my purse and after several seconds of searching, I finally found them and placed them in the palm of his hand. He helped me get into the car, closing the door behind me, and then settled himself in the driver's seat. Without saying a word, he started up the car and headed towards his house. I noticed him checking the rearview mirror several times, like he was checking to see if anyone was following us, and it made me think back to our conversation at the bar about him being the club's Enforcer.

Curiosity got the best of me and I finally asked, "How long have you been the club's enforcer?"

"So you *were* talking about me tonight," he smiled.

"I guess I really don't know that much about you," I confessed. "Until tonight, I didn't even know you had a sister."

"Not much else to know."

"Doubt that," I laughed.

I was far from drunk, but I could still feel a light buzz from the alcohol. I had so many more questions running through my head, but I kept them to myself, riding the rest of the way to his house in silence. We'd been riding for several minutes when the twists and turns of the road started to make me feel a little nauseous. I was relieved when he finally pulled into his driveway and parked the car. I quickly opened the door and stepped out, leaning against the car as I took a deep breath of fresh air. Griffin mumbled something under his breath behind me as he shut the car door and started walking over to me.

"Regretting that last shot?" he smirked.

"I guess they were right. I am a total light-weight," I laughed. Before I had a chance to move, he leaned down and slipped his arms under my legs, positioning me into a bridal hold. Feeling safe and cozy in his hold, I laid my head on his shoulder and let him carry me inside. It felt so right to be there in his arms, feeling secure like he had made me feel from the first time we'd met. He took me into the living room and gently laid me down on the sofa.

"I'll be right back. Gotta lock up," he told me before disappearing into the kitchen.

I glanced around the room and was surprised to see how beautiful it was. It had all the elements of a log cabin that I adored, right down to the cobble stone fireplace and large brown and white fur rug. The furniture was simple and masculine, yet there was a warmth to the room that made it feel like a home. Looking around, curiosity got the best of me so I decided to take a little self-guided tour. I quietly stood up and wandered down the hall. Ironically, the first room I stumbled into was his bedroom. His large king size bed looked so inviting with its thick comforter and oversized pillows. I ran my hand across the soft fabric, and I just couldn't help myself. Thinking that I would be okay if I could just lay down for a minute, I pulled off my jacket and boots and crawled into his bed. That's all it took. I rested my head on his soft pillowcase, smelling a hint of his cologne, and fell sound asleep.

Chapter 12

STITCH

A FTER I'D LOCKED up the house, I went into the kitchen to get Wren some water and two pain relievers. She'd had a good time tonight, a really good time. I liked having her at the club, seeing her loosen up a bit. Since she wasn't used to drinking, I figured that she was going to have one hell of a headache in the morning, so I went into the living room to bring her a glass of water and a couple pain relievers. When I walked back into the room, I was surprised to see that she was no longer lying on the sofa. Thinking that she might have gotten sick, I went to check if she was in the bathroom, only to find her snuggled up in my bed. Fuck. I don't know how long I stood there staring at her, marveling at how beautiful she looked lying there in my bed, before I walked over and placed the bottle of water and the pain relievers on the bedside table. Fighting the urge to crawl in next to her, I covered her up with my comforter, knowing that I needed to give her time to sleep off the alcohol. Reluctantly, I headed to the living room and turned on the TV. Some news channel rumbled in the background, but I wasn't paying any attention to what they were saying. I had other things on my mind.

I should've been thinking about the conversation Cotton and I had earlier about our upcoming meet with the Forsaken Saints. They were coming in to discuss our plans for ending this shit-storm we had going with the Pythons and whether I liked it or not, we needed their help. I also should've been thinking about Wren's predicament with Michael. I needed to get inside that man's head and figure out what the hell he was going to do now that he'd lost the only connection he had to Wren. But I wasn't thinking about either of those things. There was only one thing that was consuming my thoughts – the woman in my room, lying in my bed.

I was at a loss. I didn't know what the hell to do about her. A part of me wanted to walk into my room and devour her, claim her body as my own and show her how she'd been driving me wild all these weeks, but I couldn't move. Doubts had begun to creep into the crevices of my mind, making me wonder if this thing between us would ever work. I looked at her and all I saw was good. She was just so very fucking good, and she deserved love and kindness – gentleness. I didn't understand those things because I've never had them, except those occasional glimpses from my grandmother so very long ago. I'd long since forgotten those times. I'd become a man who didn't know how to be gentle or tender. I only knew violence, brutality, physical pain. I could do those things, I understood them. How could I go to her, be with her, when all I knew was the complete opposite of what she really was? Yeah, I was the exact opposite of someone decent, someone good. I sat there wondering if it might be possible for me to learn those things, to be those things for her. I had my doubts that I could change and after everything she'd been through, I wondered if she'd be strong enough to handle what I really was.

"Hey," she whispered from the doorway. It was almost two in the morning and she was standing there wearing one of my old t-shirts and a pair of my thick white socks. Sexy as fuck. She bashfully pulled at the hem of my t-shirt and said, "Hope you don't mind. I had to get out of those jeans."

"Don't mind at all," I answered. Looking at her in that moment, everything became crystal clear. It snapped tight in my mind. I didn't give a fuck about my doubts. I wanted her, and I was going to do whatever it took to make her mine. "How are you feeling?"

"Much better. I'm really sorry about falling

asleep on you like that. I'm not used to being out, much less having a few drinks," she started. "I was just going to lay down for a minute to rest my eyes, but your bed was so unbelievably soft. I just couldn't help myself." She smiled and started walking over to the sofa, casually sitting down next to me. I pulled the blanket off the back of the couch and tossed it over her legs as she nestled into my side. When she laid her head on my shoulder, she asked, "Whatcha watching?" Her actions were simple, no hesitation at all. It was like she'd done the exact thing with me a hundred times, feeling totally relaxed to be sitting there next to me.

"Nothing much," I told her as I passed her the remote.

A wide smile crossed her face when she took it in her hand and said, "Seriously? You trust me with the all-powerful remote. That's huge!"

"Yeah, I trust ya. Don't disappoint," I told her smiling.

"No pressure there," she teased as she started to scroll through the channels, briefly stopping on some chick flick. She looked up at me, quickly noticing my disapproving facial expression, and turned back to the TV as she continued to search through the channels again. She finally stopped at one of the older Batman movies and laughed when she said, "I hear the two of you might have something in common."

"Batman?"

"Mmm hmmm. Batman," she said, fighting back a smile.

"No... Nothing like him, darlin'."

"Yeah, you're probably right. Henley was pretty out of it when she mentioned it," she laughed. I was about to ask her what she was talking about when she said, "Don't bother asking. It's in the vault." Then she lifted the remote and changed the channel again, finally settling on some old comedy. She dropped the remote in my lap and pulled the blanket over her feet, cuddling up in the crook of my arm.

"The vault?"

"Yep," she clipped. "In the vault."

"You know I've got ways to make people talk," I warned.

"Don't use your Enforcer threats against me, mister. It's in the vault," she smirked. "Now behave."

"Easier said than done," I smiled.

She rolled her eyes playfully and asked, "What made you want to join a motorcycle club in the first place?"

"Cotton."

"How so?"

"There are people that you come across in your life that can see your mistakes, all the things you've done wrong in your life. Maybe it's the way you carry it on your shoulders or a look on your face. Not sure what it is, but Cotton has always been one of those people who just knows. Back then, he saw me for what I was, and instead of judging me, he asked me to be his brother. Joining the club gave me a place to move forward, gave me a chance to forget my past," I explained.

"You don't seem like the kind of guy that makes mistakes," she smiled.

"Made plenty. Still make them," I told her.

"Then, I'm glad that you have Cotton and your brothers. They're like your family."

"Exactly, and I'd do anything for them."

She sat there staring at me for a minute, then a goofy grin spread across her face. I knew she was still feeling her buzz when she said, "I like your beard and you have pretty eyes."

"Nothing about me is *pretty*, Wren," I scolded.

"I disagree," she laughed as she rested her head on my chest.

As we sat there watching the movie, I slowly ran my fingers through her long soft hair until she drifted off to sleep. When the movie credits started to play, I carefully pulled her into my lap, cradling her in my arms as I carried her back into the bedroom. I gently laid her in the bed as I pulled the covers over her. I had just turned to leave when she called out to me, "Don't go."

Chapter 13

WREN

HE STOPPED, FROZEN in his tracks, looking at me with an intensity I didn't quite understand. I could see the doubts raging in the back of his mind as he considered my plea, and I couldn't help but wonder what made him hesitate. There was so much about him that I didn't know, but I knew how he made me *feel*. A sense of security washed over me whenever he was near, giving me a feeling of peace that I hadn't felt in years. I trusted him. I truly did, and believe me, my trust wasn't something that was earned easily or given lightly. I knew Griffin was different. Right from the very beginning. That first time I met him in the diner, I just knew – *I knew* that he was different. He sat there in his leather jacket and with all of those tattoos talking to my son, who was looking at him with pure wonder in his eyes, and then he turned and looked at me. Suddenly, I saw past the biker – straight to the man, and like a magnet I felt a pull to him that I could not comprehend. In my gut, in my heart, I was certain that he was someone that I wanted to know. Every self-preserving instinct I had (and trust me, those instincts were finely honed) screamed that he was going to be someone important in our lives.

In just a few weeks, he'd taken my world by storm, making me feel things I never dreamed and as much as it scared me, I wanted it. I wanted him. So while I was apprehensive, it wasn't him I feared, it was the idea of a relationship that scared me. But the things I felt when I was with him weren't feelings I could ignore. Whatever was happening between us, it was something I wanted – no, I needed – to explore.

"Griffin," I urged, as I took the covers and pulled them back, inviting him to come lay next to me.

Without any further delay, he took his phone out of his pocket and kicked off his boots. His fingers dropped to the buttons of his jeans, and I watched with what I was sure were lustful eyes, as they fell to the floor. Leaving him with just a pair of form fitting boxers and his t-shirt. I nearly groaned out loud at the image he painted; he was beautiful. He was built the way a man ought to be built... tall, muscular, broad shoulders... *my god*. Just looking at him made me feel alive. It'd been a while, a good *long while* since I'd enjoyed –

actually *enjoyed*, the company of a man, and when he started walking towards me I got hot all over. He quietly settled on the bed next to me, and laid his head down on the pillow.

I rolled to my side and with my face just inches from his, I whispered, "See... that wasn't so hard."

"Only one thing hard about getting in this bed with you," he whispered with a faint growl. "Not sure I'll be able to restrain myself."

I leaned in closer to him, briefly pressing my lips to his. "You never have to restrain yourself with me."

"You don't know what you're saying."

"I do. I trust you."

"It's not that easy, Wren. Never been a gentle man. Never known... *gentle*."

I placed the palm of my hand against his chest and said, "Beneath that hard exterior lies a man with a good heart, one that fights for what is right and true. There is gentle in you, Griffin. I've seen it. I've felt it."

"I've spent all these weeks watching you, seeing that you are everything I'm not. Good. Decent. Loving. I'm none of those things and I will tarnish you with my touch. I've tried to fight it. Tried to protect you from me, from the darkness inside of me, but your pull is too strong, Wren. I want you too damn much."

"Don't fight it," I said.

Without any further hesitation, he reached for me, pulling me closer to him as his mouth found mine. An eager moan echoed through the room when his tongue brushed against mine. My hands roamed across the ridges of his chest as he deepened the kiss. He lifted himself from the bed, settling between my legs as he continued to explore my mouth with his tongue. I'd never felt such a strong desire for a man. With just a simple touch he sent a surge of heat coursing through my body, burning me to my very core. He made me feel craved, wanted beyond belief. When he looked at me, I wasn't worried about the imperfections of my body or my lack of sexual experience. I could see the yearning in his eyes and I'd never felt so beautiful.

Without saying a word he pulled his t-shirt over his head, tossing it aimlessly onto the floor. My eyes were instantly drawn to the colorful ink that marked his body and I couldn't stop myself from reaching out to touch him. He watched silently as I studied the intricate designs of his tattoos, brushing the tips of my fingers along his flesh. The artistic details were meticulously precise, obviously having taken hours upon hours to complete. I was utterly enthralled by them but was suddenly pulled from my trance when I noticed the large knotted scars hidden beneath the ink. There were so many scars.... too many to count. I looked up at him, my mind filled with questions but the words were stuck in my throat. He remained perfectly still as I continued to run my hands over his chest, feeling the various gnarled grooves on his skin. When my fingers reached his back, I gasped in horror. "Griffin?"

"Happened a long time ago, Wren," he said. His smile was almost prideful when he said, "Battle wounds of sorts."

"Someone hurt you?" I asked quietly, my voice trembling.

"Like I said, it was a long time ago," he said, giving me a thoughtful look. "Can't change the past, and I wouldn't even if I could. Every scar, every mark on my body is a reminder that I survived. Just living through it made me who I am."

I lifted myself from the bed, throwing my leg over him and carefully resting my knees at his sides as I straddled him. I lowered my head and pressed my lips against one of the larger scars that marked his chest, kissing him softly. He clearly had been through hell and back and just the mere thought of what he might have been through tore at my heart. Whatever had happened to him, he'd managed to come out on the other side with a strength and compassion that I couldn't begin to comprehend.

"If these scars made you who you are, then I am thankful for each and every one of them," I whispered. I continued kissing and caressing each of the raised welts along his skin. When I brushed my tongue across his nipple, a deep growl of approval escaped his body.

His hands reached for the back of my neck while his fingers tangled tightly in my hair as he took control of the kiss. My hips automatically rocked against him, feeling him thicken beneath me as he devoured my mouth, deepening the kiss. Desire for this man was running rampant through me, and I was losing what little control I had over my body. Any inhibitions I might have had completely washed away when he moved his hands to the hem of my t-shirt, pulling it over my head. He let out a deep breath as he took my bare breasts in his hands, holding them firmly while brushing his thumbs across my nipples. I loved the feel of his hands on my body, every touch sent me soaring into a new level of ecstasy. I felt his erection throbbing beneath me, and I was quickly becoming desperate to have him inside me.

A hiss escaped his lips as I reached down, slipping my hand into his boxers. His breathing became short and strained as my fingers wrapped around him, in a matter of seconds, I was flipped around, lying flat on my back with the weight of his body pressed against me. His mouth dropped to my ear, the warmth of his breath sending goosebumps down my spine as he whispered,

"So damn perfect."

I felt my underwear sliding along my flesh as he eased my panties down my legs. A needful moan vibrated through his chest as he gazed down upon my naked body. A devilish grin spread across his face while he settled his hips back between my legs making my entire body tremble with need. He lowered his face to my neck, the bristles of his beard tickling against my skin, as he nipped and sucked along the contours of my body. My hands dropped to his waist, pulling at his boxers to no avail. He chuckled into the crook of my neck as he lifted his hips and eased them down his legs. Seconds later they were on the floor next to his abandoned t-shirt, and his mouth was back on mine. A part of me wanted to slow down, savor the moment, but I was too far gone and just couldn't restrain my-self. I wanted him, needed him. My legs spread further to accommodate him, my hips shifting up toward him as he rubbed himself against my clit. My entire body ached for him, nearly to the point of pain.

"You sure about this?" he asked.

Unable to even string together coherent words I nodded, praying that he wouldn't stop.

"Need the words, Wren. Once I have you, I'm not letting you go."

His words caught me by surprise, but I knew he meant exactly what he'd said. Without reservation, I whispered huskily, "I'm sure, Griffin. I've never been more sure about anything." I wound my hands around his neck, pulling him closer and kissed him. It was gentle and slow, a promise. "I want this. I want you. Please, Griffin."

"You have me," he groaned. His hand slipped between us, and his fingers entered me. Each movement was meticulous and slow, causing me to writhe beneath him while his thumb brushed back and forth over my clit. I was unable to control my whimpers of pleasure as he delved deeper inside me. I didn't recognize my own voice as it echoed through the room. I was completely lost in his touch, loving the feel of his calloused hands against my body. The bed creaked as I arched my back, feeling the muscles in my abdomen tighten with my impending release. My breath caught in my throat as waves of pleasure rushed through me, and just when I thought I couldn't take it a moment longer, his hand was gone.

Griff's forehead rested against mine as he grazed his cock against my entrance. His erection, hot and hard, burned against my clit while he teased me with it. He shifted his hips to align with my opening. I gasped loudly as he thrusted deep inside me, giving me all he had to give in one smooth stroke. He froze, looking at me with a horrified expression. Grumbling curses under his breath, he said, "Don't want to hurt you."

"You didn't, and I'm not going to break, Griffin. You feel so good. Stop holding back," I demanded as I rocked my hips, begging him to continue.

His hands reached up to the nape of my neck, fisting my hair as he drove into me again. Slow and demanding, he was in complete control. Every smooth slide of his cock into my body was a statement of dominance. His teeth raked over my nipples, and I cried out wanting more. I dug my nails into his back as my whole body ignited with such intense heat, it was unlike anything I'd ever experienced before. He pushed deeper inside me as I tightened around him, and a deep moan vibrated in his throat as he picked up his pace. His control shattered, and unable to restrain himself any longer, he pounded into me in long, smooth rapid strokes. I fought to catch my breath as I felt my climax approaching. My entire body jolted and jerked as my orgasm crashed through me. I continued to tighten around his throbbing cock until he found his own release. His body collapsed on top of mine, exhausted and sweaty. I loved how he felt pressed against my bare skin, buried deep inside me. I never wanted to leave that spot.

Chapter 14

STITCH

SUNLIGHT PIERCED THROUGH the window blinds, pulling me from my sleeping stupor, but my body was resisting. I couldn't remember the last time I'd slept so soundly, and it was difficult to pull myself awake. When I finally opened my eyes, I was not happy to see that I was in the bed alone. I'd fallen asleep with Wren wrapped in my arms, and I expected to wake up with her still next to me. Fuck. I was just about to get worried that she'd left when I heard a commotion in the kitchen, followed by the rumble of profanities. Curious to see what the hell she was up to, I threw back the covers and pulled on a pair of sweats. The intoxicating smell of fresh cooked bacon made my stomach growl as I walked down the hall. When I reached the kitchen, I found Wren hovering over the stove. She was wearing another one of my old t-shirts and her wet hair was falling around her shoulders. Her face was flushed, and she was obviously flustered when she reached into the oven.

"Son of a .... God dog it!" she grumbled under her breath as she dropped the hot pan of biscuits on the counter. "What the hell is wrong with me? It's like I've never cooked stupid biscuits before," she pouted as she shook her hand wildly at her side. When that didn't work, she placed the tip of her thumb in her mouth, trying to stop the burn.

I cleared my throat and smiled. "Morning."

With her finger still in her mouth, she turned to face me. Her eyes instantly dropped to my bare chest, widening with appreciation as she stood there ogling me. Several seconds later, she removed her finger from her mouth and said, "Umm... you need to put on a shirt."

"I do?" I taunted.

"Yeah, you do. I still have to finish breakfast, and there is no way I can concentrate when you are standing there with that chest and all those muscles bulging everywhere. And don't get me started on that V thing you've got going," she said, quickly motioning her hand up and down my body. "You'll need to put on some different pants, too. Like old man pants with a big ole' sweatshirt and maybe a Dive cap."

"Old man pants?"

"*Griffin*... You *cannot* walk around here wearing those," she scolded pointing to my sweats and shaking her head.

"And why's that, Wren? Feeling a little *tempted*?" I teased, smiling at her seductively.

"Look here, Mr. *Sex* on a stick. I've made you breakfast. I went *all* out. I even made bacon and I don't *do bacon* and... go put on a shirt!" she argued.

"Okay," I chuckled as I advanced towards her.

When I had almost reached her, she started backing away and screeched, "What are you doing?"

"You're wearing my shirt," I teased. A look of a panic rushed over her face when I reached for the hem of the t-shirt she was wearing.

"Umm... Yeah, I used your shower, too," she replied as he grabbed the spatula off the counter, holding it tightly at her side.

When she shuffled her feet, my attention was drawn down to the floor, and I smiled when I saw that she was wearing a pair of my socks again. With my hands still clinging to her shirt, she popped my arm with the end of the spatula. "Back off jack!" she teased.

"Hey! I was just doing what I was told," I laughed as I grabbed the spatula away from her, tossing it back on the counter. She looked around the room, searching for her next weapon of choice. Seeing that nothing was in reach, a faint scowl crept over her face when she said,

"Are you going to behave yourself?"

"I'm not making any promises," I told her playfully. I placed my hands on her hips and pulled her closer. Her frown quickly faded when I wrapped my arms around her, holding her tightly against my chest. I never expected to like it so much – having her here, in my kitchen, making a mess while she cooked me breakfast, treating my house like a home. But I did like it. I liked it more than I ever thought I could. She had me wanting things I'd never imagined I'd ever want or need. She had me wanting a future, a future with her and Wyatt. She watched me with those beautiful black eyes as I lowered my head and claimed her mouth. The kiss quickly became heated, and a slight whimper escaped her lips when I stepped forward, pressing her back against the stainless steel refrigerator door. Her arms wound around my neck, and just as we were starting to lose ourselves in the moment, the oven timer started ringing.

She quickly pulled away from me and rushed over to the stove. A wonderful aroma filled the air when she opened the oven door, making my mouth water. I watched her pull out the breakfast casserole made with sausage, eggs, and tons of cheese, and I couldn't stop myself from stepping closer, trying to get a better look.

When she noticed me peering over her shoulder, she said, "It's my mother's recipe. I hope you like it."

"Looks incredible."

"Get yourself a plate. I'm starving," she said as she grabbed the biscuits and bacon and placed them on the counter next to the casserole. While I fixed us both a plate, she poured us each a tall glass of orange juice, then joined me at the kitchen table.

"How often do you cook like this?" I asked, taking a large bite of casserole.

"A lot, I guess. I'm always trying to find a way to get Wyatt to eat his vegetables. He pretty much hates anything healthy, so I've had to get pretty creative," she explained.

"You're a good mother, Wren."

"Sometimes I wonder," she said, shrugging her shoulders.

"He's an awesome kid, and it's obvious that he's crazy about you. You've gotta be doing something right."

"Yeah, he is pretty amazing," she said smiling. "I called to check on him earlier, and he couldn't stop talking about the science museum my mother is taking him to today. He'd spent last night researching everything about it, and I'm sure he'll drive my parents crazy with all his little facts."

"I think his facts are cool," I admitted. "And I'm sure they'll enjoy spending the day with him."

"Yeah… they always do. Don't know what I would've done without all their help," she explained.

"You see them often?" I asked, knowing I hadn't seen them around over the past few weeks.

"Normally I do, but things have been pretty hectic lately."

"You haven't told them."

"About Michael? No. I didn't want to worry them. They have enough on their plate without me adding to it."

I'd never known what it was like to have parents that gave a shit about me, so I was in no position to spout off advice to her about dealing with her folks. Deciding to leave it alone, I stood up and headed to the counter to get myself another helping. When I turned my back to Wren, I heard her take a deep breath. Unlike my chest, the scars on my back weren't hidden behind tattoos. The scar tissue was too deep, and even the best tattoo artists wouldn't attempt to cover them. I knew they looked gruesome, but they were a part of me. Nothing I could do to change it.

Before she had a chance to ask, I said, "It was my grandfather." When I turned to face her, tears had already begun to fill her eyes. "He was just a mean old bastard." I didn't bother explaining what he'd done. She'd seen the scars, there was no doubt how they'd gotten there.

"Your grandfather did all that to you?" she asked in barely a whisper.

"Mostly. Some are shrapnel scars from the war. I did two tours in Iraq, but was medically discharged before I could enlist for a third."

She stood up and walked over to me, winding her arms around my waist as she hugged me. She rested her head on my chest and said, "I hate him. I don't even know him, and I hate him for doing that to you."

Chapter 15

WREN

"WHAT ABOUT YOUR sister? Did he hurt her too?" I asked. His muscles became tense, making me instantly regret asking the question.

"No, darlin'. I would've killed him if he ever laid a hand on her," he answered. He kissed me softly on the cheek, then pulled back from our embrace as he took his plate off the counter and placed it in the sink. With his back to me, he asked, "How long are your parents planning to keep Wyatt?"

The way he'd just shut down reminded me of Wyatt, pulling back into his turtle shell. It was clear that he wanted to change the subject, and even though I had a thousand questions I wanted to ask, I let him. "I have to finish up a paper for one of my classes, so they are keeping him until tomorrow."

I started putting the rest of the dishes in the

sink, making myself busy cleaning up the mess I'd made while cooking breakfast. Griffin followed suit, and in no time, we had almost everything cleaned and put back where it belonged.

I was putting the last few dishes in the sink when he asked, "Can you do it here?"

"What?"

"Your paper? Can you do it here?"

"I guess so. My laptop is in the car, but..." I started.

"Then, do it here," he said, giving me a sexy wink. "I'll grab your stuff out of your car." And just like that, he was out the door. Seconds later, he returned carrying my laptop bag and all of my books.

"Okay, I guess I'll get to work then," I told him.

"Where do you want all this?"

"Mind if I do it in the living room? I like to watch TV while I work."

He laughed as he said, "Didn't your mother teach you not to do your homework in front of the TV."

"She tried, but it never really stuck," I admitted with a smile.

"Imagine that," he laughed. "Make yourself at home. I've got a few things to tend to, but I'll be around if you need me," he explained.

"Are you sure you want me to stay?" I asked,

giving him one last opportunity to get me out of his hair.

He stepped over to me, placing his hands on my jaw, and said, "I wouldn't have asked if I wasn't." Then he leaned in and kissed me. It was short, but effective.

With a satisfied smile on my face, I curled up on the sofa with my laptop in my lap and got busy. I already had most of the research done, so it was just a matter of actually writing the five-page paper. It didn't take me long to get most of it written, even with one of my favorite movies playing on the TV. I'd almost forgotten that I wasn't alone, when Griffin walked in the living room and sat down in the recliner next to me. When I glanced over to him, I couldn't stop myself from laughing out.

I was barely able to form the words when I asked, "What are you wearing?" I couldn't believe what he'd done. It was the funniest, crazy thing I'd ever seen.

"What?" he asked innocently. "You don't like my old man pants?"

"Griffin! Where on earth did you find those?" He was wearing a pair of ratty jeans that were at least three sizes too big, and an old Notre Dame sweatshirt with a matching Divecap.

"I don't know what you're talkin' about," he said, looking down out his outfit.

"Seriously? Griffin, this is not the sort of

thing I'd ever expect you to do," I said, trying to reign in my hysterical laughter.

"So you're saying you don't like my big ole' sweatshirt?" he asked.

"You got me... it was a bad idea, a very bad idea," I admitted as I placed my laptop on the coffee table and walked over to him, quickly pulling the hat off his head. I tossed it to the floor, and said, "Take it off."

"Not happening. Now go sit your pretty, little ass back down on that sofa and finish your paper. When you're done, I'll lose the sweatshirt."

"So you are blackmailing me now?"

"If that's what you wanna call it," he said with a sexy smirk.

Shrugging my shoulders, I headed back to my spot on the sofa and said, "What goes around comes around."

"I don't respond well to threats, Wren," he teased.

With an audible huff, I sat back down on the sofa, pulling my laptop in my lap and grumbled, "Mr. Baggy pants doesn't do threats."

I didn't have to look at him to know that he was smiling. I could feel it. His good mood radiated off him, making the entire room light. I felt so at ease with him, happy. We spent most of the afternoon just sitting in that living room, enjoying each other's company while I worked on my paper. I loved that he was so patient, and how he understood that my classwork was important me, never making me feel like I needed to rush. As the day passed, he made himself busy with odd jobs around the house, quietly working on his computer or doing small projects outside. There were a couple of times that I heard him talking on the phone, and I became concerned when he raised his voice, growling at someone on the other end of the phone about a warehouse.

Moments later, he walked into the room, and I could see that his lighthearted demeanor had disappeared. He was wearing his cut and a pair of jeans that actually fit, and his body seemed tense. Something was weighing on his mind, and his good mood was quickly fading. Feeling guilty that I might be keeping him from something, I said, "You know, you don't have to entertain me. If you have something you need to do…."

"I've got to take care of a few things," he said, forcing a smile. "Maverick and a couple of the other brothers are coming by for a minute. We'll be out in the garage, but you can call me if you need anything."

"Okay," I answered. Henley and Cassidy had already warned me about *club business*, so I knew not to ask him what was going on. It felt strange not talking about something that seemed so important to him, but I kept my mouth shut as I

watched him fiddle with his computer. His eyebrows furrowed into a scowl when he read
whatever information he'd pulled up on the
screen. Something was going on — something
that obviously concerned him, and I couldn't
help but wonder if it had something to do with
that phone call.

He was still focused on his computer when
the rumble of motorcycle engines drew his attention to the driveway. Without a word, he shut his
computer down and walked over to me, giving
me a light kiss on the lips before heading out the
front door. I could hear their muffled voices as
they greeted one another, and then everything
fell silent. Curiosity washed over me, making me
want to jump up and peek out the window, but I
stayed put. Instead, I pulled out my phone and
was surprised to see that I had several text messages from my mother.

> **Mom:** I don't want to worry you, Wren, but
> there is a strange man on a motorcycle out-
> side of the house. He seems to be watching
> us. Do you know anything about this? 10:45
> a.m.
>
> **Mom:** He followed us to the Science Muse-
> um. 1:35 p.m.
>
> **Mom:** Your father is about to go out there
> and ask him what he is doing. 2:15 p.m.
>
> **Mom:** Your father asked him. He wouldn't

tell him anything. Said he was just doing what he was told to do. 2:35 p.m.

Mom: Your father was out there talking to him for a very long time. He thinks they are friends now. 2:36 p.m.

Mom: I think I should call the police. 2:38 p.m.

I had no doubt that Griffin had something to do with the biker in the driveway, and the last thing my mother needed to do was call the police. Thankfully her last text was just a few minutes ago, so hopefully there was time to stop her before she made the call. The phone only rang once when she answered, "Hello?"

"Mom, don't call the police," I demanded.

"Wren, this man has been sitting out there for hours, and he's not the only one. I've seen other of these motorcycle men come and talk to him. It's strange," she explained. "Do you know these men?"

"Uhh... yeah, I do."

"Are you going to tell me who they are?" she pushed.

"They are just trying to keep an eye out for Wyatt, Mother. It's not a big deal." I knew the minute those words came out of my mouth that I'd just said the wrong thing.

"Not a big deal? Seriously? There are men on motorcycles sitting in my front yard, Wren. They look like those men from those movies, and I'm pretty sure he has a gun. Then your father goes out there and talks to him, like *he* can do anything about it," she huffed. "These men look *dangerous!*"

"I'm sorry. I know this is hard to believe, but I trust them. They are going to make sure that Wyatt is safe. That's all you really need to know," I explained.

"Safe? From what?"

"I don't want to worry you about all ...."

"Wren, I am your mother!"

"Yeah... and you've got enough to worry about with Grandma Pip and Dad's retirement. There's no point in me..."

"Wren Mathis, you know that you and Wyatt mean the world to me. I worry about you even when everything is fine. It's *who I am*, so if there's something going on, tell me."

I spent the next twenty minutes telling her everything that had happened over the past month with Wyatt and Michael. The news did not surprise her, and she pleased to hear that Wyatt's visitation with him had been suspended. When I started talking about Griffin, she became oddly quiet, and I wasn't sure what to make of her silence. I started to become anxious, worrying that she would have something negative to say about him. Until that moment, I hadn't realized how important it was to me that she liked him. I hated that it mattered so much to me, but the fact was... it did.

When I finished talking, there was a brief moment of silence before she said, "You care for this man."

"Yeah, I do," I answered. "He's so good with Wyatt, and there's something about him that makes me feel safe. I don't know how to explain it."

"You've been through so much, darling. Michael put you and Wyatt through hell, and he's still doing it. Even though he's made it difficult, you've managed to make a life for you and my precious grandson. You've done everything you could to make sure that Wyatt has everything he needs, and it's time for you to do the same thing for yourself. If you think this man will make you happy, then maybe you should give it a try. Just be careful," she explained.

That was not what I expected her to say. A smile slowly began to spread across my face when I said, "Thank you, Mom."

"I love you, sweet girl. I just want you to be happy," she started. "I don't know what to make of these young men on motorcycles, but I think it's best that you keep them away from your father. You should've seen the way he was looking at that man's bike. Wren... he's too old to be riding on one of those things."

"You're probably right," I laughed. "I better

get going. I need to finish up this paper, but I'll check back with you later on tonight before Wyatt goes to bed."

After I hung up the phone, I spent the next half-hour finishing up my assignment. Once I was done, I emailed it to my professor and shut-down my laptop. Just as I was putting everything away, Griffin walked through the front door. I could see by the expression on his face that his mood had improved considerably. There was a hint of a smile on his face when he asked, "You finished with your paper?"

"Yep. All done."

"Good," he said, as he took off his cut and laid it over the back of the chair.

"I just talked to my mom."

"Yeah?"

"She was asking me about a biker that was parked outside of their house. You wouldn't happen to know anything about that, would you?" I asked.

"I might," he said as he made his way over to the sofa and sat down next to me.

"You know, a heads up would've been nice. Mom was a little freaked out," I explained.

"Probably should've mentioned that," he admitted. "Sent Q' over to keep an eye on Wyatt."

"Well, my dad seemed to really like Q'," I told him smiling.

"Is that right?"

I leaned forward, kissing him lightly on the lips before I said, "Thank you for making sure my son is safe. You don't know how much it means to me.

"Can't say that every decision I've made has been the right one, but looking after Wyatt... there's no doubt I did the right thing there. He's an amazing kid, and his mother, she knocks me off my feet."

"You think so?" I teased.

Without saying a word, he reached for me, pulling me into his lap. He pressed his lips against mine, kissing me with a passion that made my body tremble.

Chapter 16

STITCH

T HE MINUTE HER lips touched mine, everything else immediately faded away. It was
just her and me, and nothing else mattered. I
loved the way she felt in my arms, so fucking
perfect. I couldn't get enough of her. Her breasts
pressed against my chest as I claimed her mouth,
fueling my need for more... I had to have *more*.
Her eyes filled with wonder as I eased her back
down to the sofa, slowly lowering her lacy panties down her long, slender legs. I needed to taste
her, sweet and warm. With her eyes still locked
on mine, my hands traced along her legs, gliding
tenderly over her calves to her knees, pushing
them apart, as my hands skated up her inner
thighs. My thumb brushed back and forth across
her clit, tormenting her with a barely-there touch.
She lifted her hips, pushing against my hand as
she tried to increase the pressure.

"Been thinking about having you like this

since I saw you standing there in my t-shirt. Couldn't even concentrate on what my brothers were saying, knowing you were in here waiting for me. Can't stand it a minute longer," I told her as I pulled my shirt over my head. I lowered my mouth down between her legs, and she gasped when my tongue skimmed across her clit. I teased back and forth in a gentle rhythm against her sensitive flesh, loving the way her body instantly reacted to my tongue. Her fingers delved into my hair, gripping me tightly as her hips squirmed below me. Her breath became ragged and short when I thrust my middle finger deep inside her, twirling against her g-spot with a slow and steady pace. I added a second finger, driving deeper, sliding farther inside her. She tensed around me as her body rocked against my hand. I smiled against her flesh when I noticed the goosebumps prickling across her skin, loving my effect on her. I continued to nip and suck the inside of her thigh, just inches away from her clit. Her hips lifted up from the sofa, begging for me to give her more. I instantly drove my fingers deeper inside her pussy, caressing her delicate flesh. Her body shuddered beneath me as I began to fuck her with my fingers. She released my hair, and her hands dropped to the cushions of the sofa, digging into the fabric as she started to tremble uncontrollably.

"Oh my god, Griffin," she shouted as her head thrashed from side to side. I continued to curl my fingers inside her, teasing that spot that was driving her to the edge as I licked her clit. She murmured my name over and over as the walls of her pussy clenched around my fingers. She was still in the throes of her release as I dropped my jeans to the floor. I slipped on a condom and settled between her legs, pulling her closer to the edge of the sofa. She looked so fucking beautiful, looking up at me with intensity in her eyes. This woman was getting to me in a way that I'd never expected; I was falling for her, falling fast and hard. Her eyes sparked with need when I hovered over her, brushing my cock across her clit. She didn't move; she laid there, legs spread around my hips, just begging to be taken, and my heart stopped beating in my chest. Fuck! I couldn't imagine wanting anything more as my cock pressed against her entrance. With a devilish grin, she shifted her hips, forcing the head of my cock inside her. Unable to resist, I thrusted deep inside, then stopped just long enough for her to adjust to me.

"Never knew," I whispered in her ear as I slid her t-shirt up over her stomach, revealing her perfect round breasts. "I never knew it could feel this good." I took her nipple in my mouth, and I felt her breath quicken as my teeth raked across her flesh.

"Yes," she moaned, her legs instinctively wrapping around my waist as she pulled me deeper inside her. I slowly withdrew, then gradually eased back inside her. My pace was steady and unforgiving, and she took it, wanted it even. She was everything I needed and more. My eyes roamed over her, taking in every inch of her gorgeous body. Her chest rose and fell as she tried to steady her breath, each gasp of air sounding more desperate than the last. Shifting her hips upward, her tight pussy gripped firmly around my cock. I growled with satisfaction when I felt her squirming beneath me. My pace never faltered as I continued to thrust inside her, over and over, constantly increasing the rhythm of my movements.

"Fuck!" I shouted out as my throbbing cock demanded its release too fucking soon. I wanted to take my time with her – memorize every move, every whimper – but she was just too fucking tight, felt too fucking good to stop. I plunged inside of her again and again, feeling her pussy spasm with her release. My hips collided into hers, my thrusts coming faster, harder with every breath I took. I looked down at her, amazed that she'd been able to reach me, break through my walls and make me feel so strongly for her. She made me a better man just being around her, and I wanted to be everything for her. Wren's body jolted as her orgasm riveted through her body. Hearing the light whimpers of my name echoing through the room sent me over the edge, and I couldn't hold back any longer. I was done holding back. She was mine in every way.

When I stood, her legs fell limp against the cushions of the sofa. I eased down, carefully lifting her into my arms and headed down the hall towards my bedroom. She looked up to me and cleared her throat before saying, "I'm... gonna need... a minute before ... we do that again."

I laughed and gave her a light kiss before sitting her down on the edge of the bed. I left her just long enough to start a hot bath. When I walked back in the room, she said, "I don't think I'll be able to move my legs for the rest of the night."

Smiling, I lifted her back into my arms and said, "Means I did something right."

"You did *lots* of things right," she smirked.

Laughing, I carried her into the bathroom and lowered her into the tub. Once she was settled, I eased in behind her. She rested her back on my chest, relaxing in the warmth of the water. After several minutes, she said, "I could get used to this."

"I know the feeling," I told her as I ran the washcloth along her shoulders.

"I wish we could stay like this... lock the rest

of the world out, and get lost in our own little world for just a little while longer."

"We've still got tonight. We'll make the most of it," I told her as I kissed her shoulder.

She turned back and looked at me as she asked, "Could we stay in tonight? Maybe order some pizzas and watch a movie."

"Yeah, we can do that," I answered, thinking there was no place I'd rather be.

"Then you could do that thing you did again."

"What thing?" I asked laughing.

"Any of those things you did in there earlier," she smirked.

After we got out the tub, we spent the night curled up on the sofa eating takeout pizza and watching movies. When the second movie ended, I took Wren to bed and happily did all those things that she wanted me to do to her. The sun was just starting to rise when we finally drifted off to sleep. We'd been asleep for several hours when my phone started to ring. When I didn't answer, it rang again. Realizing it was actually my burner ringing; I pulled myself out of bed and grabbed my phone off the dresser.

"Yeah," I clipped.

"Need you back at the clubhouse now," Maverick announced.

"We got a problem?"

"Fireworks at the construction company," he

started.

"Fuck!" I shouted.

"When Guardrail went to see about it, several guys tried to break in on Al. Two Bit and Lil' Ricky were there to handle things, though."

"They were after Al. Those fireworks were just a decoy to get Guardrail out of the house."

"Yeah, that's what we figured. Cotton is calling for a lockdown, and the meet with the Forsaken Saints has been moved up. They'll be here in less than two hours."

"I'm on my way. Gotta take care of some things first," I explained.

Chapter 17

WREN

"SLOW DOWN, GRIFFIN. And remember who you are talking to. I don't know what the hell a lockdown is, and I certainly don't know what it has to do with Wyatt or me," I snapped.

"I don't have time to explain it all to you right now. We've got to go get Wyatt, and go to your house to pack your things."

"And what happens after that?" I demanded to know.

"You'll stay at the clubhouse for a while. It's the only way we can make sure you both are safe,"

"Safe from what? What is going on?" I cried.

"It's nothing for you to worry about. You're gonna need to trust me on this," he answered as he pulled up his jeans. "We don't have much time."

I tossed the covers back and reluctantly got

out of the bed. Searching feverously around the room, I tried to find my clothes. "How long do you think this will take?" I asked as I started to get dressed.

"As long as it takes," he answered. He was already dressed and waiting by the door as I put on my boots. "Let your folks know that we'll be there in twenty minutes."

My emotions were running wild, and I couldn't tell if I was scared out of my mind or just flat out pissed. One minute I was in a peaceful slumber with Griffin by my side, and now I was being dragged out of the bed and told that I was going to be locked in their clubhouse. None of it made any sense, but I knew something was wrong. The sound of Griffin's voice when he was talking on the phone worried me – actually it petrified me. His anger was palpable, instantly changing him into a man I didn't even recognize.

Sensing my trepidation, he walked over to me and pulled me close as he said, "It's going to be okay, Wren. I need you to trust me on this."

He'd never given me a reason not to believe what he was saying, so I said, "I do trust you, Griffin."

"Then, let's go get Wyatt." He kissed me lightly on the lips, then took my hand and led me out the door. We didn't talk on the way to my parent's house. I couldn't even if I wanted to. It was useless; I couldn't form a single clear thought. My mind was filled with too many questions, and the look on Griffin's face wasn't making things any better. His fingers were gripping the steering wheel so tightly that I thought it might crumble beneath his hands. When we pulled up in the driveway, my mother rushed outside to greet us.

With a big smile on her face, she met us as we were getting out of the car. "You're so early," she complained, giving me a quick hug. When Griffin came up behind me, she extended her hand and said, "You must be Griffin. I've heard so much about you."

"Nice to meet you, Mrs. Clayborn," Griffin told her as he shook her hand.

"You've made quite an impression on Wyatt. He hasn't stopped talking about you, and I'm pretty sure my daughter feels the same way," she said playfully.

"*Mom*," I scolded, shaking my head with embarrassment.

"It's true," she continued. "I asked him about Griffin after our little talk."

Before she had a chance to say anything else, I asked, "Where's Wyatt?"

"He's inside with your father. He can't find his tennis shoes."

I was just about to go in and help when they both walked out the front door. "Hey, Stitch," Wyatt said excitedly, completely oblivious that I was standing there. He walked over to him and asked, "Where's your motorcycle?"

"It's back at the clubhouse," Griffin answered.

"I wanted Papa to see it," Wyatt told him. He quickly turned back to my father and said, "It's really cool, Papa. It's a Harley, and it's got double barrel exhaust pipes. You really gotta see it!"

"Maybe some other time," my father piped in. "I'm Stan. Heard a lot about you," he chuckled as he shook Griffin's hand.

"I told him how Wyatt's been talking about him," my mother said smiling.

I thanked him as I took Wyatt's bag from my father and said, "I wish we could stay longer, but Griffin has some things he needs to take care of. Thank you for keeping him this weekend."

"Anytime, sweetheart. You know we love having him here," my mother said as she gave me a quick hug. "Have a good week, Wyatt."

"I will," he told her, giving her a little hug before he darted for the car.

I walked over to my father, and just as I was about to give him a hug goodbye, he said, "Wyatt thinks a lot of this fella, and from the look on your face, you do, too. Just be careful." He wrapped his arms around me, hugging me tightly as he whispered, "Love you, sweet pea."

"Love you, too, Daddy," I told him.

When we got in the car, Griffin pulled out

his phone and called someone at the clubhouse. "Need you to meet me over at Wren's house. You'll need to help her get her stuff loaded and back to the clubhouse while I go to the meet." There was a brief pause, and then he said, "Good. We'll be there in ten."

As soon as Griffin hung up his phone, Wyatt asked, "Are we going somewhere, Momma?"

"Yeah, buddy. We're going to go over to Griffin's clubhouse to stay with him for a few days. The bug man is coming to spray, and we need to be out of the house for a couple of days," I explained. Normally such news would throw him off balance. He needed time to adjust to changes in his routine, but he seemed to like the idea.

"We get to stay there… at his clubhouse?" he asked excitedly.

"Yeah, bud. We do."

"That's awesome. Can I take my game?" he asked.

"Sure. And anything else you'd like to bring," Griffin answered. "And there'll be some other kids there you'll get to meet. Dusty is about your age, and he loves video games, too."

"Okay," Wyatt said smiling.

When we pulled up to the house, there was a motorcycle parked in the driveway. We all got out of the car, and one of Griffin's brothers walked over to us. I remembered seeing him at the club the other night. He was a little younger than Griffin, and unlike most of the others, he wasn't sporting any facial hair. I wanted to run my fingers across his cheek to see if it was as smooth as it looked. Then, he seemed so nice, sporting a big, bright smile, but today he looked different. Today, he had the same serious expression that Griffin was wearing, making him seem a little intimidating.

When Griffin noticed me looking at his brother, he cleared his throat and said, "This is Clutch. I had him come over so he could help get you packed. I've got to get back to the club."

"You're leaving?" I asked.

"Don't have a choice here, Wren. I'm the club Enforcer, and my club needs me right now. Clutch is one of my brothers from the club, and I trust him to take care of you both. Once you get your things together, he'll get you over to the club where he can watch over you and the other women."

"Okay," I agreed.

"Hey, Clutch," Wyatt said. "That's a cool road name."

"Thanks, little man," Clutch told him.

"I've got to get over to the clubhouse. Prez wants all the officers at the meet. Just make sure they get the necessities and get gone," Griffin ordered.

"No problem. Cotton gave me my orders.

I've got it from here," he told Griffin. "And you can just take my bike back to the clubhouse. I'll ride with them."

Before he left, Griffin walked over to me and said, "You with me on all this?"

"I'm with you," I answered, lifting up on my tiptoes and quickly pressing my lips to his. When he turned to leave, my stomach dropped and my chest grew tight with worry. I had no idea what he was about to face, and the thought of losing him filled me with dread. Watching him walk towards that bike made my anxiety skyrocket to an unbearable level. "Griffin!"

He quickly turned around and before he could say anything, I rushed over to him, hugging him tightly. "Please be careful. I don't know what is going on, but I don't want anything to happen to you."

He wrapped his strong arms around me, holding me tightly against his chest, and said, "Wren, it's going to be okay. Nothing's going to happen to me."

"Promise?"

"I'll be waiting for you back at the clubhouse," he said. He stepped back, releasing me from his embrace and said, "I've got to get going."

"I know. I'll go pack," I told him as I turned and headed towards the front door. I heard the motorcycle engine roar to life just as I was closing the door and before I even had a chance to think, Wyatt came running towards me.

"Do you know where my socks are?"

"Umm... I think they are on the dryer," I told him. "I'll get them."

"And I need my good pajamas... and my slicky pants and pullover... and my..." he started.

"I'll get everything. Just get your suitcase out of the front closet and take it to your room. I'll be in there in a second to help you," I explained.

Clutch was amused by Wyatt's excitement, laughing under his breath as he watched Wyatt race back to his room. "He's pretty stoked about all this, isn't he?"

"You have no idea. Once he gets there, he may never want to leave," I laughed. "Griffin doesn't know what he's gotten himself into."

"I think he does, and he seems pretty happy about it. You need any help with anything?" he offered.

"Not yet. Just make yourself at home," I told him. "And if you're hungry, there's some food in the kitchen."

"Want some coffee?"

"I'd love some. Thanks," I told him as I headed for the laundry room. Once I'd bundled all of Wyatt's things in my arms, I started towards his room to help him put everything in his suitcase. When I walked in, he had all of his clothes and games in neat little stacks on his bed. "Got the rest of your clothes. Why don't you put them in your suitcase while I go get my things together?"

"Okay," he answered.

I went into my room and opened my closet door, trying to decide what I needed to pack. Since I didn't know how long we'd be there, I had no clue how much I needed to take with me. After mulling everything over, I decided to stick to the basics – jeans and t-shirts. I grabbed what I could fit in my suitcase and started loading it in my bag. When I was almost finished, I decided to go check on Wyatt's progress.

Just as I was walking across the hall, I heard a man's voice coming from the kitchen. It was low and husky, and even though I couldn't hear what he was saying, something about it sent chills down my spine. Clutch roared back at him, and seconds later, I heard a thunderous bang. I'd never heard one up close, but I knew it was a gunshot. I stopped frozen in my tracks as pure panic washed over me. My first thought was to get to Wyatt; I needed to make sure that he was okay. I was headed towards his room when I heard Clutch call out to me.

"Run!" he shouted.

My breath caught in my throat when I heard another gunshot explode through the house, followed by the sound of footsteps charging in my direction. I slammed Wyatt's door, locking it behind me. Adrenaline pulsed through my body as I hurried to pull his dresser in front of the door.

"Wyatt, I need you to come over here. I'm going to help you out of the window, and then I want you to run. Don't look back... just *run!*" I pleaded as I opened his window.

The doorknob clicked back and forth, and when it didn't open, a booming thud echoed through the room as someone tried to kick down the door. My breath quickened as I reached over for Wyatt.

"Momma, who is that?" he cried. His little body trembled as I lifted him into my arms. I eased him out of the window, and just as he feet were about to hit the ground, I saw him. His face was distorted with rage as he stole Wyatt from my grasp.

"Michael, *NO!*" I cried.

Chapter 18

STITCH

I WAS NOT a fan of lockdowns. Having everyone crammed in close quarters for days was not my idea of a good time, but the thought of having Wren and Wyatt there actually had me looking forward to it. I was ready to get the meet over with so I could help them get settled. I hated leaving them back at the house, but I trusted Clutch to make sure they got here with everything they needed. When I pulled into the lot, the club was already rumbling with activity. The families were coming in, unloading their cars as they prepared for the days ahead. Along with them, the brothers from the Forsaken Saints had turned up even earlier than expected. But that was a good thing – meant they were eager. We were all ready for the shit with the King Pythons to end, once and for all.

When I walked in, the bar was packed. The brothers were all gathered around talking, waiting for Cotton to call church. I glanced around the room, watching the women scurry around the room making sure all the guys had what they needed. Cassidy was at the bar with Dive, the Forsaken's Sergeant of Arms, and they both looked pretty fucking cozy sitting there talking. I shook my head and thought Cotton would have a field day if he caught sight of them. But then again, Cass was smart – she knew Cotton would be pissed to see her talking to him. Dive was a good guy as far as I could tell, but I wasn't going near whatever shit-show Cass was starting. Scanning the room, I spotted Guardrail was sitting at one of the tables in the back, so I headed over to ask him about Allie.

Before I had a chance to speak, he said, "She's rattled, but she's doing fine."

"And the construction company?" I asked.

"We put the fire out before it got out of control. It'll take a little work, but we'll be back up and running in a few days," he explained.

"Why Allie?"

"Doesn't matter. Going after her like that was a big fucking mistake," he growled. "I'll kill those motherfuckers with my bare hands for even thinking about touching her."

The bar instantly fell quiet when Cotton walked in. With a slight nod towards the back door, he let everyone know it was time for church. Just as he was turning to leave, he spotted Dive and Cass. He glared at them for a long moment, making Dive's eyebrows furrow in momentary confusion. With a quick glance over to Cass, Dive realized how he'd fucked up. He didn't say a word as he stepped away from Cassidy, looking at her like she had three heads and followed his brothers into church.

It didn't take long for everyone to fill the room. Rip took a seat next to Cotton, while Dive and the rest of his brothers stood behind him. Once the rest of us were settled, Cotton turned to Rip and said, "Appreciate you coming in early like this. We needed to make sure that everyone was on the same page before these motherfuckers strike again."

"Not a problem, but it's been pretty quiet on our end," Rip started. "Been waiting for them to make a move, especially with all that intel they gathered on our brothers and families."

"Came after us again last night. That's why we moved the meeting up. Used explosives to set a fire at our construction company. Figured they did it to lure out our VP, so they could get to his old lady."

"Fuck!" Rip growled.

"We managed to get her out before they could get their hands on her, but the attempt was made nonetheless," Cotton explained.

"Making a move like that, they're calling for war," Rip told him.

"You got that right. We've had Big Mike looking into their club, identifying all their possible allies. They've got the numbers they need to make one hell of an attack," Cotton replied.

"Any idea where they might be holed up?" he asked.

"Mike caught something on one of our surveillance streams last night. Looks like a couple of them are hiding out in one of the old warehouses in Angeles, waiting for more to come."

"There's no doubt that there will be more. We can count on that, but you've got us. Been allies with your club for as long as I can remember, even back when your uncle was sitting in that chair. Best thing he ever did was passing the reigns down to you. Just let us know what you need," Rip confirmed. "But if they have the kind of numbers I think they've got, you're gonna need more than just us at your back."

"Aware of that," Cotton answered. "Already talked to the Northern Caballero's. They're in."

"And with the Nomads we know in the area, we'll be able to take them on," Maverick added.

"We're armed and ready. I suggest you do the same," Cotton warned.

"Been ready. We'll head over to the warehouse now and secure the perimeter. Just let us know what you want us to do from there," Rip assured him.

"Thanks, brother. We're right behind you,"

Cotton told them as they stood to leave. When the last of the Forsakens had pulled out of the gate, I set out to find Wren and Wyatt, figuring they were getting settled in their room by now. As soon as I walked through the door, I got a bad feeling as I scanned the room and didn't see any sign of them. I reached in my back pocket for my phone and called Clutch. I called three times, but he didn't pick up. It wasn't like him not to answer, confirming my thoughts that something wasn't right.

Not wanting to waste any time, I headed straight to my bike. I'd almost made it to the parking lot when Maverick stopped me. "Hey, what's the rush? Is something going on?"

"Wren and Wyatt aren't here, and Clutch isn't answering. Headed over there now to see what the hell is going on," I told him, trying not to panic.

"I'll go with you," he told me as he motioned for Q' and Two Bit to follow us.

When I pulled through the gate, I didn't look back to see if my brother was behind me. I knew he was there, same as Q' and Two Bit; they were always there when they were needed. Maverick could see that I was worried, but there was no way he knew just how panicked I really was. Not knowing what was going on with Wren was killing me. I tried to push it out of my thoughts, trying to block the 'what ifs' that were racing through my mind, but it was useless. I knew in my gut that something was wrong, really wrong. I turned the throttle forward, pushing my bike to its limit. I didn't care how fucking dangerous it was to drive at that speed, I had to get there. When I finally pulled up to her house, her car was still parked in the driveway. I got off my bike and hurried inside. When the door swung open, I found Clutch sprawled out on the floor, bleeding out all over the kitchen. Maverick and the boys came in behind me. Each of them rushing over to help with Clutch.

"Oh *shit!*" Q' blurted out.

Maverick dropped to his knees and placed his fingers at Clutch's throat, checking for a pulse as he tried to talk to him. "Clutch... brother, I need you to open your eyes. Can you do that for me, man? *Open your eyes*," he demanded.

With a strained moan, Clutch tried to say, "Wr...en."

I knelt down over him, and inches from his face I pleaded, "What is it, Clutch? You gotta tell me."

When he tried to take a breath, his face grimaced in pain, but he finally managed to say, "Her... ex, and..."

"And what, Clutch?" I shouted as I tried to get him to respond, but it was too late. He'd passed out from the pain and blood loss.

"Call Doc and get the brothers to bring over

a cage," Maverick told Q'. "Tell them to make it fast. He's lost a lot of blood."

While Q' made the call, Maverick did what he could to stop the bleeding. Clutch had two gun-shot wounds to the chest, one close to his shoulder and the other was lower by his hip. Doc had dealt with much worse, so I had no doubt that he'd be able to help him. He'd have to.

"I'll be right back," I told him.

He nodded, and I headed down the hall to see if there were any signs of Wyatt or Wren. When I passed Wyatt's room, I noticed that most of his things were gone. He'd packed up most of his stuff, but there was no suitcase. I left his room and walked across the hall to Wren's. Her suitcase was still laying on the bed, but there was no sign of either of them in the house. I went back to Maverick and said, "No trace of them. That motherfucker came in here and took them!"

"Just stop for minute. Take a step back, and think about this. This is your thing, Stitch. You've gotta treat this like it is anybody other that Wren and Wyatt, forget that this is about the people you care about. It's the only way you're going to be able to find them," Maverick explained.

I rested my back against the wall and took a deep breath. I knew he was right. I was letting my emotions get in the way. I tried to clear my thoughts, think only of the facts that I knew about Wyatt and Wren and all of their dealings with Michael. I was trying to think, but it was damn near impossible with my brother laying there on the floor, looking paler by the minute. Thankfully, the cage finally pulled up out front to get him. Two Bit opened the door for Doc, leading him quickly over to Clutch. Once Two Bit helped Doc load him in the SUV, they were both gone, leaving me alone with Maverick and Q'.

When they pulled out of the driveway, Maverick turned to me and said, "Okay, brother. How do we find this kid and his mother?"

"The cell phone. I gave him a cell phone a couple of weeks ago. It has a tracker in it," I remembered.

"I'll call Mike," Maverick told me.

"What do you need me to do?" Q' asked.

"Just hold tight. Once, we know what direction they're headed, we're going after them," Maverick answered.

I paced back and forth, glancing periodically over at the pool of blood on the kitchen floor. Each time I saw it, the more infuriated I became.

"Stitch," Maverick warned.

"I know," I growled. He just didn't get it. He had no fucking idea. He had a family – Henley, Gavin, and for most of his life, he had parents that gave a shit. I'd only had Emerson, and now, for the first time, I had a chance for more. I had a chance to know what love really was, to truly feel it and give it back in return. I couldn't lose it. Not now, not when I was so close. Wren was mine, and I wasn't about to let anything happen to her.

"They're out on 101 headed towards Clearwater. About an hour out," Q' announced.

"Want me to call Gonzalez? See if he can help us out?" Maverick offered.

"I'll call him," I told him as I walked out the front door and headed towards my bike. Before I started my engine, I dialed Gonzalez's number. The Caballero's were our allies, and Gonzalez owed me more favors than I could count. It was time for him to pay up.

"Yell-o?" Gonzalez answered.

"Need your help," I told him. "Blue 2007 Toyota is coming through your area. Need you to stall him."

"Got an ETA?" Gonzalez asked.

"Any minute. Be ready. Coming in on 101 headed to Clearwater. Slow him down," I demanded.

"On it brother."

"Good. I'm on my way," I told him as I hung up my phone and started up my bike.

Chapter 19

WREN

EVERYTHING HURT. AN excruciating, throbbing pain pulsed through my head, making it difficult to make a clear thought. I had no idea where I was, but my head was in such a deep fog that I couldn't even make myself try. It was hard to breathe, my lungs burned with every single breath like someone was sitting on my chest. I just wanted to lie there, wait for the pain to go away, but something was gnawing at me. I needed to wake up. I had to wake up, but it was just too hard. I couldn't move, couldn't think. I had no idea what was going on with me.

Breathe.

Slow... steady.

Damn. Why was it so hard to breathe? I inhaled through my nose, trying to keep my breaths short and shallow, so it wouldn't hurt so much. It didn't help. Nothing helped, and the darkness was pulling at me. I was about to just give into it, when it came to me. The one thing that could pull me out of my haze... Wyatt. My chest tightened with panic, making my lungs burn even more. When I tried to move, a pain shot to my side, reminding me of the time that Michael had broken my ribs during one of his meltdowns. I stilled myself and tried to call out to Wyatt, but only muffled cries echoed around me. When I tried to move, I realized that my arms were bound behind me. I called out again, but something was covering my mouth. Duct tape was sealed across my lips, another reason it was so hard to breathe. I could feel my heartbeat pound against my chest as panic washed over me. I was losing it. I needed to focus.

Breathe.

Slow... steady.

I couldn't fall apart. Not now, not when Wyatt needed me. I twisted my wrists back and forth, trying to loosen the ties around my hands. Ignoring the pain, I rocked my body from side to side and quickly realized that I was confined in some kind of box or maybe the trunk of a car. Not only was I bound and gagged, I was locked away, all alone.

Alone.

I felt like the walls were closing in on me. I couldn't stop the panic from setting in as the memories came rushing back. My heart started to beat rapidly in my chest as I thought back to the night Michael had locked me away in that damn closet. It was just once, but it made a lasting impression on me. I'd told him I was going to a movie with a friend. When I headed towards the door, he slapped me... hard. Before I had time to react, he pushed me into the closet and kicked me in the side with his boot when I tried to fight back. Seconds later the door slammed shut, and not only did he lock it, he propped a chair against the doorknob to ensure that I couldn't get out. He had a thousand reasons why he'd gone to such an extreme, but that night I'd seen the light. There were no limits to Michael's abuse, and the thought of my son being alone with him scared me to death. I had to get to Wyatt before Michael hurt him. Nothing else mattered. I fought against my restraints again, determined to get my hands free, but it only made it harder for me to breathe with that damn tape across my mouth.

Breathe.

Slow... steady.

I moved my wrists slowly, back and forth, until I felt my skin begin to tear against the rope. I stopped and rested for a few minutes before trying again... and again... and again. After what felt like forever, I finally started to feel the rope give around my wrists. Blood trickled down my hands as I twisted them back and forth, making them slippery. It was just enough for me to pull one hand through the rope, letting it fall free around my other hand. I quickly lifted my hand and removed the blindfold and the tape from my mouth. I laid back and took a long, deep breath, letting my eyes adjust to the dark surroundings. I was no better off without the blindfold; I still couldn't see a thing.

I tried to lift myself up, but the stabbing pain in my head forced me back down. I reached up along the back of my neck, searching for the source of pain. I carefully ran my hand over the large knot on the back of my head, and blood covered my fingertips. I was bleeding, but it wasn't bad enough to keep me down. I had to get the hell out. I had to get to Wyatt. I felt along the curved edges of the wall, and I quickly determined that I was indeed in the trunk of a car. Now, I just needed to find a way out.

Chapter 20

STITCH

As soon as we pulled into Clearwater, I pulled over and gave Gonzalez a call. "What's the word?"

"I got 'em," Gonzalez told me over the phone. "Got lucky when the prick stopped for gas. Added a little agua to his tank when he went in to buy a pack of cigarettes," he laughed.

"Where is he now?" I asked.

"Guess they figured it was gonna take 'em a while to fix his car, so they gave him one of their rentals. Followed him to the hotel down on Lumbar Street. It's gonna take 'em a few hours to fix his car, maybe longer if Dan isn't working in the garage today. His son, Billy, don't know shit about engines. It could take him forever to figure out it was just water in the tank," Gonzalez laughed.

"Did you see who he had with him?" I asked.

"Yeah. Had a kid in the backseat."

"You didn't see a woman with them?" I asked.

"Nah, just the kid from what I could tell," he answered.

"I'll be there in five. Make sure he doesn't go anywhere," I demanded.

"Sitting right outside his room, brother. This guy ain't going nowhere. He's been in there cussing and screaming for the past fifteen minutes. Just came out to the car and grabbed himself a fifth of bourbon, so it won't be long 'till he'll settles down," he chuckled.

I didn't like the sound of that, not one fucking bit. I knew very well what Michael was capable of, and I hated the thought of Wyatt and Wren in the room alone with him.

"If he starts in again, distract him," I ordered.

"You got it," he chuckled.

Wren should've been in that car and not knowing where she was gave me a sick feeling in my gut. When I couldn't shake the feeling, I made a call to Cotton. As soon as he answered, I asked, "Need eyes on the warehouse. Gonzalez didn't see Wren with Michael."

"We're here now," Cotton confirmed.

"Have you seen any sign of her?" I asked anxiously.

"Not yet. Only one of the cameras is still working, and there has been no sign of anyone coming or going since last night. We're securing the perimeters before we go in," Cotton explained.

"Fuck," I roared. "We need to get in there. See if she's there!"

"We've gotta be careful with this Stitch. Don't know how many guys they've got with them," Cotton started.

"There's no time to be careful. They might have Wren!" I let out a deep breath and said, "You just gotta see where I'm coming from here, Cotton."

"I know damn well where you're coming from, but you need to reign that shit in, brother. We're playing this thing smart. Period," he answered.

"I'm claiming her, Cotton," I told him. "I can't lose her."

"And you won't. If she's there, we'll get her," he assured me. "First, we get eyes on them... see what we're up against. Then, we'll make our move."

"Understood. I'll be there as soon as I can," I told him before I hung up the phone.

With Maverick and Q' following behind me, I pulled back on the highway and pushed the throttle forward. I couldn't stop thinking about Wren, and the way that she looked at me when we were standing in her driveway. Until that moment, I hadn't been sure how she truly felt about me, but seeing her standing there, pleading with me to come back to her... I knew. And knowing I felt the same way about her, I was even more determined to get to her. I sped through traffic, weaving through the cars that lined the street. Even though Gonzalez was there to keep an eye on things, I couldn't stop myself from thinking the worst, and by the time we pulled into the hotel parking lot, I was on the brink of losing it. As soon as I parked my bike, I headed over to Gonzalez. He was standing under the stairway smoking a cigarette, and he hadn't changed a bit since the last time I'd seen him. His hair was slicked back, and he was wearing his cut with his handgun noticeably tucked away at his side.

"Long time no see, brother," he smirked. "Yo, Maverick, good to see you, man."

I had no intention of wasting time with small talk, so I looked over at the door behind him and asked, "Is that the room?"

"Yeah, it's been pretty quiet for the last few minutes," Gonzalez told me. "This guy's a real asshole, if you ask me."

I nodded and made my way over to the door. I took a deep breath and knocked. When I heard a commotion inside, I covered the keyhole so he couldn't see me standing there. After several seconds, Michael called out, "What do you want?"

"Room service. Got you some extra towels,"

I answered. With one good shove, I could've knocked the door down, but I didn't want to frighten Wyatt. I had to be patient. As soon as the door opened, I reached in and grabbed Michael by the throat, lifting him off the ground as I hauled him outside. He tried to fight against my hold, but then, I reared back and slammed my fist into his gut, completely knocking the breath out of him. He barreled over as I shoved him towards Maverick. "Hold on to him," I ordered as I walked into the hotel room, quickly searching for Wren and Wyatt.

At first the room looked empty. The bottle of bourbon was resting on the table next to the bed, and the TV was blaring with some old war movie. After checking the bathroom, I was about to go back outside when I finally saw him. Wyatt was crouched down in the corner, partly hidden by the window drapes, and he was cautiously cradling his arm in his lap. My gut twisted into knots when I caught sight of the swelling and bruising forming on his obviously broken wrist. I couldn't take it. Seeing him look so damn scared, all balled up in that corner took me right back to that godforsaken barn. All the hell I'd been through came rushing back to me, and I wanted to scream for it to stop. I didn't want to remember, didn't want to think about how I'd spent night after night terrified out there in that fucking barn. I loathed that feeling of being weak and scared and so fucking alone. I wanted those feelings gone, to stay forgotten. But there sat Wyatt, feeling exactly the same way I'd felt all those years ago. Rage coursed through my veins, and I had to fight the urge to slam my fist through the wall. I took a deep breath trying to push back the anger, knowing the last thing I needed to do was scare him even more. He didn't even notice me standing there as he stared down at his arm.

"Wyatt?" I called out to him.

His head quickly lifted, exposing more cuts and bruises on his face, and when his eyes met mine, tears began to roll down his cheeks. "Stitch! You came! I knew you'd come," he cried.

He tried to stand, but grimaced with pain when his arm shifted to the side. Before he had a chance to try again, I rushed over to him and picked him up off the floor, carefully sitting him down on the bed next to me. I glanced down at his arm and asked, "Your dad do that to you?"

"Yeah... it hurts," he cried. "I tried to get away from him so I could get back to Momma. But, he grabbed me and held on real tight. I think he broke it," Wyatt whimpered. "I want my momma."

When he mentioned Wren, my gut twisted with worry. "Do you know where your momma is, Wyatt?"

"N-no," his voice trembled as the tears continued to pool in his eyes. "I'm scared something happened to her, Griffin. What if my daddy hurt her?"

"She's going to be fine. I'm going to make sure of it," I promised. Fuck. If she wasn't with them, then where the hell was she? There was only one person that knew, and he was outside with Maverick. Before I could get my hands on Michael, I needed to get Wyatt to the hospital. "I want you to wait here for just a minute. I'm going to see what we can do about your arm. Okay?"

"No!" he cried. "Please don't leave me."

"I'm not leaving you. I'll stay right here in the room, okay? I'll stand at the doorway... it won't take long," I told him.

"Okay," he agreed.

I was so torn. I knew Wren was out there, needing me to find her, but I couldn't leave Wyatt, not when he was hurt like this. I knew better than anyone how scared he must be, and I wasn't going to leave him until he was ready for me to go. In the meantime, I had to trust that my brothers would be able to find Wren and that they'd protect her until I was able to get there.

I stuck my head outside the door, looking for Gonzalez and found Maverick standing there with Michael's face crammed against the side of the building. He had a childlike smile on his face as he held Michael's arm firmly behind his back, obviously enjoying himself. I nodded in approval, then motioned over to Gonzalez to come to the doorway. When he approached me, I asked, "Got a hospital in this town? The kid has a broken wrist that needs to be tended to."

He let out a breath of smoke from his cigarette and nodded. "Yeah. Got a surgeon we use from time to time over at the county hospital. She'll let us bring him in without asking a bunch of questions. I'll call one of my boys to bring a cage over," he offered.

"Good. Thanks, brother," I told him.

Maverick looked over to me and asked, "Did you find out anything about Wren?"

"Not yet. Wyatt doesn't know where she is," I growled, glaring over at Michael.

"Tell ya what... we'll take care of the kid, while you tend to his dad," Gonzalez smirked.

"You're wasting your time. I don't know where that bitch is!" Michael panted. "And Wyatt's fine... not a damn thing wrong with him. He's just a pansy assed little shit," Michael shouted as he tried to pull himself free from Maverick. Grabbing a fistful of Michael's hair, Maverick pulled his head back and slammed it into the brick wall.

Noticing the blood dripping from Michael's nose, I told Maverick, "Take him around back. I don't want Wyatt to see anything." I looked over to Q' and said, "I'm gonna need you to go with us to take Wyatt to the hospital. I want someone I can trust to be there with him after I leave."

"Not a problem," Q' assured me.

"That kid in there means something to me, brother."

"Understood."

Once Maverick and Michael disappeared around the back of the building, I went back over to Wyatt and knelt down in front of him. His eyes grew as big a saucers when I said, "My friend Gonzalez is going to take us to the hospital so we can get your arm looked at. Once we know everything's going to be okay with your arm, I'm going to go find your momma.

"Do you know where she is?" he whispered.

"No buddy. I don't, but I'm going to find out."

"What about my dad? Do you think he knows where she is?" he asked.

"Yeah, I think he might, so I need to go talk to him for a little while."

"My dad isn't very nice."

"Already know that Wyatt. It'll be fine. Let's get that arm taken care of."

"You think I'll get a cast?" Wyatt asked. I thought he was nervous about getting a cast until he smiled and said, "I've always wanted one. Maybe I can get a blue one like Thomas had last month when he broke his elbow."

"Yeah. I figure you'll get yourself a pretty

cool cast out of the deal. And when you're all fixed up and the doc's finished, Q' will take you back to the clubhouse."

"I've got my bag packed. It's in the trunk of Dad's car," he explained.

"I'll take care of it," I told him. A car horn blew outside, letting me know that Wyatt's ride had arrived. "They're here. You ready to go?"

"I'm ready," he answered. He slowly stood up and walked over to me, carefully wrapping his good arm around my waist as he gave me a light hug. "Thank you for coming for me, Stitch."

Never realized how much a simple hug could mean to me. Having him there in my arms and knowing that he was going to be okay, healed a part of me that I didn't even know was broken. Without thinking, I leaned down and kissed him lightly on top of his head. After a few seconds, I knelt down and lifted him into my arms, carefully carrying him out to the car.

Once I had him settled in next to Q', I headed over to my bike and followed them to the hospital. Thankfully, the doctor was waiting at the backdoor for us when we pulled up. As soon as she saw his wrist, she had him rushed to x-ray. When they returned, she let us know that his wrist was broken, but it was a clean break. She wouldn't have to set his arm, and he'd only need to wear a cast. Relief washed over me when I realized he was going to be okay.

I turned to him and said, "Looks like you're going to get that cool blue cast after all." Then, I cleared my throat and said, "Wyatt, I'm gonna need you to do me a favor."

"What kind of favor?"

"I need to get going now. I need you to hang here with Q' while the doctor finishes fixing you up so I can go see about your momma. Can you do that for me?" I asked.

"Yeah, it's alright. I like Q'," he answered. Just before I turned to leave, Wyatt called out to me, "Griffin?"

"Yeah, buddy?"

"Please find my momma," he pleaded.

"I'll find her. Don't worry," I assured him. So much time had gone by, and I was beginning to worry that I might be too late. The thought of losing Wren tore at my heart in a way that I couldn't comprehend. In such a short time, I'd come to feel things for her that I didn't even know was possible for a man like me. I wanted her... needed her... loved her.

I looked over to Q' and said, "Call me as soon as you get done."

"You got it," he answered, smiling down at Wyatt.

I rushed back to the hotel, and when I walked back into the room, Michael was sitting on the edge of the bed with his hands bound behind his back. Maverick gave me a disgruntled look and said, "He isn't talking."

"He will," I told him, slamming the door behind me. I placed a crowbar on the table, and Michael's eyes grew wide as he stared at it. I took a step forward, crowding him as I roared, "Where is she?"

"Already told you. I don't know where that stupid bitch is," he grumbled. "I went to the house and got my son. As soon as I had him, I left."

I took a step forward, stopping just inches from his face, and glared at him. I could smell the fear rolling off of him. Men like him loved to make themselves feel strong and mighty by feeding off of the weak, but he was no fool. He knew I wasn't weak. He knew I could kill him with my bare hands, and even though he didn't want me to know it, I could see that he was scared out of his fucking mind. "I'm going to ask you one last time and then things are going to take a very different turn here, Michael."

"Fuck you! You don't scare me," he snarled. "You're just a piece of shit in a cheap leather jacket. You're wasting your fucking time. I don't know where she is and wouldn't tell you even if I did."

"You will," I warned.

"Why do you even care? Why would a man like you want a tight ass like Wren in the first place? You get plenty of easy pussy where you come from," he snickered.

"You made your choice," I told him calmly. I reached behind him, cutting the rope that restrained him and set him free. He quickly stood, thinking that I was actually letting him go, but he was wrong... so fucking wrong. When he took a step forward, I reared my fist back and quickly slammed it into his throat, causing him to instantly start gasping for air. When he stumbled back, I grabbed his wrist, twisting it firmly behind his back until I felt it crack against the pressure, crushing his broken bone in my hand. His knees buckled to the floor as he cried out in pain. When I released his hand, he quickly pulled it to him, holding protectively against his chest.

"You know, I've seen their records," I snarled, kneeling down closer to his face. I grabbed a fistful of his hair, forcing him to look up at me and said, "Now, you've got the same broken wrist that you gave to Wyatt." I released his head and reached for the crowbar I'd laid on the table, hitting him in the side with enough force to break several of his ribs. When his body dropped to the floor, I told him, "Now, you've got the same broken ribs you gave Wren."

"Please..." he gasped.

"Oh... there's plenty more, Michael. I know every broken bone... every cut... every fucking scrape. So *tell me*, Michael. Did you stop when they begged you to stop or did you keep at it?

Did you keep hurting them, time and time again?" I asked, slamming the end of the crowbar into his now broken ribs.

Blood trickled from his lips as he cried out again, "Please, I'll tell you where she is. Just *please stop.*"

Chapter 21

WREN

W HILE I LAID there trying to catch my breath, my mind wandered back to the night I found Wyatt at that diner with Griffin. I'll never forget how shocked I was to see them sitting there together talking like old friends. Under any other circumstances, I would've been freaked out to see Wyatt with a man like Griffin, with all of his bulging muscles and tattoos. But, for whatever reason, I didn't freak, at least not like I should have. It really didn't make any sense at the time. He should've made me feel intimidated or nervous with his leather jacket and thick beard, instead I felt safe... I felt like maybe I'd been the one that was lost and finally had been found.

From the very beginning, I instinctively trusted Griffin. If there was any way that he could be there for Wyatt, he would be, but there was no way for me to be sure that Griffin was with him now. I just couldn't wait any longer. I had to get to Wyatt, I had to make sure that he was safe. Using the tips of my fingers as my guide, I felt along the edges of the trunk, searching for anything that might help me find a way out. I couldn't find the emergency release, so I only had one other option and that was to kick my way out. It took some careful maneuvering with my aching side, but I managed to wedge myself sideways. I placed my feet on the back of one of the seats and pushed with all my might. Nothing. When that didn't work, I started kicking it, over and over again. I used all my strength, all my will, and kept on trying. I focused on the right side of the seat, continuously hitting it in the same spot until I finally felt it give a little. It wasn't much, but it was enough to encourage me to keep on going. My side pleaded with me to stop, but I was determined to get the hell out of that damn car. After countless tries, the seat finally broke free. A dim light trickled in from the crack, guiding me out of the back of the car.

I exhaled and inhaled again, trying to bite back the pain as I inched my hands down to my sides and pushed myself out of the backseat. Every muscle in my body hurt when I crawled out, and once I put my feet on the ground, my head swam with dizziness. I felt my stomach tighten as the nausea hit me, so I quickly leaned my back against the car door, trying to make my head stop spinning. I wiped the blood from my brow with hands that were already sticky with dried blood, and when I glanced down at my wrists, I was horrified to see the deep cuts and tears on my skin. I was a complete mess, but I was out.

When I looked around, I realized that I was in some kind of garage or warehouse. It was an old metal building filled with various cars and trucks, and there were large wooden crates stacked along the back of the building. Even though there was a loud hum of a heater running, the place was freezing cold, and it reeked of gasoline and oil. As I scanned the area, I didn't see any tools or machinery like there would be in a garage, only wooden crates... lots of wooden crates. Curiosity got the best of me, so I walked over to see if I could peek inside one of them. The slats were nailed shut, but I was still able to use the tips of my fingers to move the straw, uncovering the barrel of a gun. When I did the same to the next crate, there was something different hidden beneath the straw. There were several squares wrapped in brown paper that were completely covered in cellophane, reminding me of packages of drugs I'd seen on TV. Feeling anxious, I quickly replaced the straw and took a step back. When I almost tripped over one of the smaller crates, I noticed a door in the back of the building. I started towards it, but stopped when I saw a light coming from an office upstairs. I stood there staring at it, wondering if it might lead me to Wyatt somehow. Even though my first thought had been to just get the hell out of there while I still could, I couldn't leave – not when there was a chance that Wyatt might be up there, or at the very least a phone so I could call Griffin. Either way, I had to find out.

With the hairs standing up on the back of my neck, I slowly crept up the long metal staircase, and I was almost halfway, when I heard a man's voice. I stopped, frozen with panic. My heart raced in fear, making me feel dizzy all over again. I held tightly to the rail as I stood there listening, trying to hear what the man was saying. It didn't take me long to realize that it wasn't Michael's voice that I was hearing. The man had an accent, and there were other men in there with him.

"Their cameras still working?" one of the men asked.

"Checked the one outside by the back gate. Made sure they saw us coming in last night," someone answered. "When are the others gettin' here?"

"They'll be here in 'bout an 'our," one of the men answered with a thick accent.

"How many are they bringing with them?" another voice asked.

"Twenty 'r so," the man answered. "Maybe more if they can round them up."

"Good, we'll need 'em, especially when their enforcer finds out that we got his girl. Would've been even better if we had the VP's, too. Get them both where it hurts for killing Victor," he growled. "Motherfuckers think they can kill our Sergeant of Arms without blowback? Hell, I can't wait to put a bullet in his head."

"Won't be long before he comes running for her. I don't figure it will be much longer before he figures out that the guy bitchin' about wanting his son doesn't have her," a man explained.

"And we'll be ready. Couldn't have made that work out any better if we'd tried," one of them grumbled. "The father gave us just the distraction we needed to pull this thing off."

"Just so we're clear, their enforcer takes his last breath tonight."

Alarms started going off in my head, screaming at me to get the hell out of there. I had to find a way to warn Griffin and let him know that he was in danger. I raced down the steps, praying that I wouldn't fall as I headed for the back door I'd spotted earlier. I slowly eased it open and slipped outside, trying to keep the door from making any noise. Once it shut behind me, I started to run. I needed to find a phone or at the very least, a decent place to hide. As soon as I made it over to one of the large metal containers, someone grabbed me and pulled me into the dark.

Chapter 22

STITCH

H E LAID THERE, cowed down on the floor, and I had to fight the urge to kick the motherfucker again. It took all I had to restrain myself but I knew killing him wasn't an option, at least not yet. "Where is she?"

"They've got her," Michael stammered.

"Who is *they*, asshole," Maverick barked.

"I don't know... I'd been waiting for Wren to come home all weekend... stopped by there a hundred times looking for them, but she wasn't home. She finally showed up this morning... I just wanted to talk to her... try to work something out, but these guys... they pulled in behind me. Jumped out of some black pickup and p-pointed a gun at me and threat – threatened to kill me," he stuttered. "I told them that I... I just wanted my son... that they could have Wren."

I clenched my fists at my side and growled, "Fuck!"

"Then what happened?" Maverick pushed.

"I waited outside. They went in to get her. I think they might have shot somebody. I just wanted to get the hell out of there, so when I saw Wren helping Wyatt out of the ww-indow, … I gr-grabbed him. I saw one of those men come up behind her, and they hit her on the back of the head, *hard*. Knocked her out cold," he explained.

Rage surged through me, and I couldn't restrain myself any longer. I slammed my fist into the side of his face, almost crushing his jaw and shouted, "Where did they take her?"

His hand immediately went to his jaw. Blinking his eyes with panic, he stared at me as he tried to regain his composure, then he answered, "I don't know. Once I had Wyatt, I left. They were still there when I pulled out of the driveway."

"Gonna need more than that, you piece of shit. How many were there? What did they look like?" Maverick snarled.

"There were three of them. Looked a lot like you… leather vests and one of them had a big snake tattoo on his arm," he muttered. "That's all I know."

"They have her. Call Cotton and let him know," I told Maverick.

"On it," he told me as he stepped outside to make the call.

I looked down at the piece of shit lying on

the floor, tempted more than ever to put a bullet in his head, but something stopped me. Even though in my mind he didn't deserve to live, he was still Wyatt's father. I was just about to start in on him again when my burner phone started ringing. I quickly pulled it from my pocket and saw that Cotton was calling.

"We've got her. She's good. Keeping her with us until it's safe to get her out," Cotton explained.

Relief washed over me as I said, "Thanks brother. Leaving here in ten."

"We're on the west side of the warehouse. Meet us there," Cotton ordered before he hung up the phone.

I shoved my phone in my back pocket before I nudged him with my boot and said, "Right now, you're still breathing. You drag your sorry ass back to that car and get the hell out of town. If you come near Wyatt or Wren again... call them, look at them, hell if you even think about them... that will be your end!"

"I got it. I'll do what you say. I won't come back," he assured me.

"Just in case you have any second thoughts," I said, throwing several pictures at his feet. "You might want to take a look at those." He took the pictures in his hand, and his face went white, as he looked at all the intimate pictures of him with his married neighbor from across the street, along with several shots of him buying drugs out on the eastside of town. "Is that where all the *anger* comes from Michael? The drugs… your need to wail on Wren and knock around Wyatt comes from the fact that you're gay and don't want to accept it?" I growled. "You afraid your folks will cut you off if they find out?"

"It's not… what it looks like," he stammered.

"It's exactly what it looks like, Michael. You've been trying to pretend you're something you're not, but there's no more hiding. No more pretending," I told him as I placed a small recorder in Michael's hand. With trembling fingers, he pressed the play button, and the sounds of his voice came barreling out of the small device:

"Stop your fucking whining! I'm sick of hearing it, Wyatt! What the hell is wrong with you? Why can't you just grow the hell up and stop acting so fucking weird?"

A loud slap followed by a muffled cry echoing through the room, letting Michael know that there was actual proof that he'd been hurting Wyatt.

"You need to pull your head out of your ass and start living in the real world." A commotion rumbled in the background, sounding like Wyatt had just been pushed to the floor. "If you go crying to your momma about this, there will be hell to pay… for both of you. Now, get your ass up before that fucking Mrs. Daniels comes in here to take you home. That bitch is going to try to rat me out for drinking a goddamn beer but she has another thing

coming! No one is going to tell me I can't see my own fucking kid."

Hearing it again made my stomach turn. The sight of Michael repulsed me, and I'd like nothing more than to beat the hell out of him all over again. But I didn't have the time to waste on the piece of shit. "Father of the fucking year asshole," I growled at him as I grabbed the recorder out of his hand.

"How do I know you won't do something with all this... that you won't show my folks?"

"You don't, and if you ever want to see your son again, you better get your shit straight," I bellowed. Without another word, Michael crawled to his feet and managed to wobble out of the room, just barely making it to his car.

As soon as he was gone, I reached for my phone, checking my messages. I had one from Q':

Q': All done. Heading back to the clubhouse now.

I shoved my phone in my back pocket and headed for my bike. So much time had been wasted, making the ride to the warehouse even more agonizing. I couldn't get there fast enough. I needed to see for myself that Wren was really okay. I knew the Python's would come after me for killing Victor, but using Wren to do it was a mistake they'd soon regret. It was my fault that Wren was taken, and I'd be the one to make these motherfuckers pay for getting her involved.

By the time Maverick and I arrived, the sun had set, and a light fog was settling over the water, making it difficult to see. I spotted my brothers' bikes several yards away from the warehouse. After parking next to them, we headed towards the west end of the building, trying our best to avoid the lights that lined that dock. It was quiet – too fucking quiet. I pulled out my phone and was just about to text Cotton, when I heard, "Griffin?"

I turned back and was stunned to see Wren standing there off to the side with Cotton, and even in the dark, I could see that she was bleeding. The side of her head and wrists were covered in blood, causing me to wince in the knowledge that she'd been hurt. I wanted to go to her, hold her and comfort her, but I stood there, just staring at her. I was so fucking relieved to see that she was okay, living... breathing, but the fury that was raging through me in that moment made it impossible to move. The thought that someone had hurt her clouded my relief at seeing her and replaced it with an all-consuming anger.

"Griffin!" she cried again as she rushed over to me, wrapping her arms tightly around me. I held her close, letting the warmth of her touch calm me, and when my anger began to subside, I pulled her back so I could get a better look. But after only a few seconds, I found myself pulling her right back to me, holding her tightly against my chest. I didn't want to let go. I needed to feel her body pressed against mine until my soul was convinced that she was truly okay.

I was still holding her when she asked, "Wyatt? Is he really okay? Cotton said you found him."

"He's going to be fine," I told her as I released her once again. "'Q' is taking him over to the clubhouse."

"Thank you," she cried. "I don't know what I would've done if something had happened to him."

"Wouldn't let anything happen to him or you, Wren. And just so you know, Michael won't cause any more trouble. He's done."

"*What?* What do you mean, he's *done?* What did you do?" she asked hysterically.

"I let him know what would happen if he came back around," I growled.

"And Wyatt? Does that mean he doesn't have to see him anymore? It's really over?" she cried.

"It's over. Wyatt won't have to see him, not unless he decides that he wants to, and only if that asshole gets his shit together." The sight of the dried blood on her flesh sickened me, and I could feel the rage beginning to build again as I reached for her hands. Glaring at the rips and tears along her wrists, I growled, "What the hell did they do to you?"

"I'm fine, Stitch. It's just a few cuts and scratches. I did most of it myself when I broke out of that stupid trunk," she explained with her voice trembling.

"They had you in a fucking trunk?" I snapped.

"Stop. None of that matters right now," she started. "We've got to get out of here!"

"Not until I kill every last one of them for hurting you," I roared. She gave me a questioning look, obviously surprised by what I'd just said.

"You can't go in there. I've already told Cotton that they're expecting you. These men knew you'd come for me, Griffin. That's why they took me, so you'd come looking. They want to *kill* you. They think you killed some guy named Victor?"

Cotton stepped over to us and said, "Need to get her back to the clubhouse. Two Bit and Stix can take her."

When I nodded, Wren fussed, "You've got to come, too! You can't go in there, Griffin. Don't you get it? I'm scared to death something might happen to you."

"This is something I've gotta do, Wren."

"But why? Why would you put yourself in jeopardy like that? What is so damn important that you have to go in there right now?" she started, but quickly stopped and stared at me with a pleading look. "Did you? Did you kill that guy... the one they were talking about?"

When I didn't answer, she grew pale. A twisted look of horror crossed her face when she realized that what they'd said was true. I had killed Victor, and I had no intention of denying it. He was a piece of shit that killed my brother, and he deserved to die. She could see my answer written on my face and was about to say something when gunfire exploded from the warehouse. I pulled her close to me, and with my gun aimed at the back door, I pulled her towards Two Bit. Wren whimpered when one of the Python's started advancing towards us. She gasped and the muscles in her body stiffened with shock when I pulled the trigger. Her body trembled in my arms when his body fell to the ground. I tucked her behind me, her chest against my back, as I tried to shield her from the gunfire. Once I'd reached Two Bit, he pulled her from my grasp and with Stix guarding them both, he rushed her to the main road where our bikes were hidden.

I stood there watching until I knew they were gone and no one had followed them. With the memory of Wren's horrified expression still on my mind, I went back to find my brothers, determined more than ever to end things with the Pythons once and for all.

Chapter 23

WREN

MY MIND WAS reeling while I sat there on that cold metal counter, waiting on Doc. Apparently I was going to need stitches for the cut on my forehead, and Doc would need to check my ribs. It was the first time I'd been alone to think about everything that had happened, and it was all too much to comprehend. I'd been knocked out, *kidnapped*, locked in some guy's trunk, and managed to get away, only to discover that Griffin had killed a man. No, strike that. He'd killed more than just one. Hell, he killed someone right there in front of me, and god knows what he did to Michael. My throat tightened, and I could feel the tears building behind my eyes. I fought it. I didn't want to cry, knowing that if I started I wouldn't be able to stop. Wyatt was waiting for me, and I didn't want him to see me upset.

Upset.

Upset was the biggest understatement of the year. I felt like my world had just stopped spinning, like everything I'd ever thought to be true was wrong. There was no denying it – I was in love with Griffin. I'd given him my heart, and he was a killer. He didn't even blink an eye when I asked him about killing Victor, like he hadn't done anything wrong. I didn't understand it. The time we'd spent together made me think that he was a man I could share my future with. I couldn't stop myself from smiling when I thought about him walking into that living room wearing that crazy outfit. I loved that he was able to be playful with me, and that he could open up to me about his past. When we'd made love, I felt a connection to him that I'd never experienced before, and I knew in my heart that he'd felt it too. He was good to me... and to Wyatt, showing me a love that I'd never known. He looked after my son, made sure he was safe, and I trusted him. But the question still remained – could I accept him for who he was, the good and the bad?

I'd been waiting for twenty minutes before Doc came in. He was an older man with kind eyes and a warm smile. There was something about him that instantly set me at ease. He stepped closer, examining the laceration on my forehead and said, "Looks like you got pretty banged up tonight."

"Little bit, I guess," I admitted.

"Gonna need to give you a few stitches," he said as he gave me a shot to numb the area. "Heard you got away all on your own."

"Not exactly," I laughed, but stopped when I felt him start to stitch my wound.

"Ballsy move busting out of that trunk like you did," he told me as he continued to work on me.

"I guess. I didn't think much about it at the time. I was just trying to get to Wyatt," I laughed. "How is he doing?"

"He's got a few bumps and scratches, but he's going to be just fine. Pretty excited about the new cast he's sporting," Doc said smiling.

"Leave it to Wyatt to be excited about wearing a cast. I give it a week. I doubt he'll feel the same way when that thing starts to itch." I felt him close off the last stitch, and then he covered the wound with a small bandage.

"Probably not," he said as his hands dropped down to my ribs, checking for any breaks. "They aren't broken, but they're pretty bruised. You're going to be sore for a couple of days. I'll give you some pain relievers and something to help you sleep."

"Okay," I answered. "Hey... what about that guy that came to my house? I think his name was Clutch. Can you tell me how he's doing?"

"Ah, it'd take more than a couple bullets to

get that guy down," he chuckled. "He'll be back on his feet in a couple of days."

"Good," I told him. Feeling overwhelmed, my gaze dropped down to the floor as I thought about another man being shot. He was a friend of Griffin's, and he'd been shot while trying to protect me.

"What's with the look?" he asked.

"I don't know. It's all just a lot to take in," I admitted.

"It is, but don't make this into something it's not," Doc told me. "Been in the club since I was Stitch's age. Met my wife and raised my children here. We're all one big family... actually a better family than most folks have. Some pretty rough times have rolled through here, but sometimes you gotta go through hell to get to the good. And Wren, there's a lot of good in this place. You've got a good man that cares a lot about you and your son."

"I know," I told him. "It's just hard to believe that a man like Griffin could actually kill someone. It's just a side to him that I didn't expect," I grimaced.

"He didn't just go out and kill someone for shits and giggles, Wren," Doc scolded. "These people that he killed... have raped, beaten and killed members of our family, and he did what he had to do to protect us. He's got the ultimate job as our protector... we all trust him with our lives," he explained.

I took a second to let it all sink in, trying to understand and accept everything he'd just said. After all I'd been through with Michael, I couldn't imagine putting Wyatt or myself in any further danger, but deep down I knew Griffin was nothing like Michael. From the very start, he'd only been kind, protective and loyal to both of us, and from everything Doc had just told me, he was the same way with his brothers.

"I guess Henley was right about him after all... he is like Batman," I muttered to myself.

"You're all set. Let me know if you need anything else."

"Thanks for patching me up... and for explaining things a little bit," I told him with a smile.

"Anytime, darlin'. Wyatt's out in the TV room with Dusty watching some cartoon," he told me.

After taking two pain relievers, I walked out of the small room and into the main hall, searching for Wyatt. I didn't really know my way around the clubhouse yet, so it took me a little while to find him. He was sitting on the sofa watching a little blonde haired boy play a video game. Wyatt was completely enthralled with the game, but the minute he spotted me, he jumped up from the sofa and rushed over to me as he shouted, "Momma!"

The power of Wyatt's hugs never ceased to amaze me. As soon as he wrapped his arms around me, all of my worries seemed to just fade away. "Hey there, little buddy."

He hugged me tightly and said, "I knew he'd find you. He promised that he would, and he did."

"Yeah, he did."

"He found me, too, and he took me to get my arm fixed," he told me as he pulled back to show me his cast. "It's blue like the one Thomas had."

"Looks pretty awesome," I smiled, thinking that Griffin had pulled through once again. Not only had he saved Wyatt from Michael, he'd taken him to the hospital, taking care of him when I couldn't.

"You think Griffin will sign it for me?"

"I'm sure he'd love to."

"Are you hurt?" he asked, looking at the bandage on my head and wrists.

"I'm fine. Just a few scratches. Who's your friend?" I asked, trying to distract him.

"That's Dusty. He's been showing me all these tricks that some girl named Henley taught him," he explained. "They're pretty cool."

"I'm sure they are. Have you had anything for dinner?" I asked.

"Dusty's mom made us some chicken nuggets," he smiled. "There was macaroni and cheese, too, but it wasn't as good as yours."

Laughing I said, "Good, I'm glad you got something to eat, but it's getting late. It's about time for you to get into bed."

"Ah, Mom. It's not that late. Just a little while longer. *Please*," he pleaded.

"*Please*," Dusty shouted from the sofa.

"You win," I answered. "Ten more minutes, and then it's off to bed."

I sat down on the sofa next to Wyatt and listened to Dusty explain all the different tricks he'd learned. The pain relievers were starting to kick in, so I rested my head on the back of the sofa, resting my eyes for a minute. I tried my best to stay awake, but with the calming sounds of the boy's voices chatting back and forth made it too hard to resist. I'm not sure how long I'd been asleep when Henley came in and woke me.

"Hey there, sleepyhead," she smiled. "How ya feeling?"

"Pretty good considering," I answered as I looked around the room for Wyatt.

"I sent the boys to put on their pajamas and brush their teeth. Hope that's okay."

"Thank you." I rubbed the sleep from my eyes and asked, "What time is it?"

"It's almost ten," she answered, looking down nervously at her watch.

"I must have dozed off," I told her. "Have the guys made it back yet?"

"No, and it's starting to worry me a little. We haven't heard anything from them since Two Bit brought you back, and that was hours ago."

A surge of panic rushed over me when I thought about Griffin being at that warehouse in the middle of all that gunfire. I couldn't stop myself from asking the same questions over and over in my head. Why didn't he leave with me? Why would he put himself in danger like that? I knew the answer. It was simple, really. He couldn't leave. Leaving would make him something he's not... the kind of man who'd walk away, and after listening to everything that Doc had said about him and his life at the club, I was beginning to understand why. Griffin's very existence was defined in being there for others, protecting his brothers and protecting those that couldn't protect themselves, and he would never walk away from that. And if I was being truthful, it was the very thing that I loved most about him. He'd been there for us all along, ultimately protecting us both from Michael and his endless abuse, and I knew deep down that he'd always be there.

Chapter 24

STITCH

G ETTING WREN TO safety had only taken a
few minutes, but when I returned, a full-on
battle had ensued. An adrenaline rush instantly
kicked in as I listened to the bullets whip past
me, tearing into the terrain around me. An elec-
tric energy filled the air, making me even more
eager to get into the mix. A lust for revenge
washed over me as the image of Wren's blood
covered face and hands flashed through my
mind. I wanted to fight – I *needed* to fight. These
men had put my brothers through hell over the
past few months, and the fact that they had
kidnapped or attempted to get Wren only fueled
my desire to take them down even more.

The fact was wars like these, men fighting for
their own perceived truth, were messy and chaot-
ic, and they never went as planned, making them
almost impossible to prepare for. That's actually
what I loved about them. I was all about the hunt

and kill, seeking my revenge for the unpunished sins of my enemy. I moved forward into the darkness of the night searching for my brothers' location, but it was difficult to see. There was a haze of fog drifting over the warehouse as the clouds billowed in off the water, looming forward as if they were searching for their next prey. It was as if they were urging me forward as I finally made it over to Cotton and my brothers.

Cotton gave me the once over, checking to make sure that I was free from any bullet wounds and asked, "You good?"

After I nodded, he said, "Rip and his crew have already secured the perimeter surrounding the east side of the building."

"What do you need us to do?" I asked.

Cotton turned to Guardrail and ordered, "Take Boozer and a couple of prospects with you and see if you can get eyes on these mother-fuckers. I want to know every move they make."

With that, Guardrail led Styx and Smokey off to find a safe place to scan the area. Boozer followed close behind, covering them as they moved into their new location. Just as they were about to be in the clear, Smokey was pinned down by a round of gunfire, forcing him to drop to the ground. Boozer and I both shot off several rounds, giving him a small reprieve to crawl to safety. Once he was hidden behind one of the large cargo containers, he gave us a chin-lift, thanking us for helping him out.

"We gotta get closer. Can't see a damn thing from here," Maverick grumbled as gunfire continued to explode around us. When Cotton nodded in agreement, I pulled out my second gun, feeling the adrenaline pumping through me as it rushed through my veins like an intoxicating drug.

Leading the way, Cotton motioned for us to follow him behind the last row of cargo containers. After loading my clip for the third time, the Pythons' causalities were building. We continued to push forward, dodging the bullets that snickered through the air. Realizing that we were gaining ground, several of the Pythons left their positions, trying to stop our advance. When a bullet struck the wall above Cotton's head, my instincts kicked in, forcing me out of the protective shield of the cargo carrier. After I had only taken a few steps, someone lunged out at me as he tried to stab me in the gut. Without hesitation, I grabbed his wrist and quickly punched him with a killing blow to the throat. He gurgled and arched his back as he choked for air. After several seconds, his lifeless body fell backwards onto the rocks.

While I was standing there under the light of the main warehouse, I noticed Styx laying on the ground and rushed over to him, pulling him behind the large loading crane. I searched his body for wounds. He'd been shot in the chest, and he was struggling to breathe, and in a matter of seconds, my leather jacket was drenched in his blood. Styx was still clinging to his gun in desperation, unwilling to stop fighting for his brothers. He was still holding on to that damn gun as he let out his last breath. His body fell lifeless in my arms.

"Fuck," I shouted as I eased him to the ground.

The deafening sounds of gunfire erupted around me, but my focus was still on my fallen brother. When a bullet pierced my flesh, a stabbing pain shot through my arm. I swallowed the burning sensation, letting my mind shut down the thoughts of how much it hurt as I lifted my gun. Firing off round after round, I stalked towards the shooter until his body dropped to the ground. Once I was sure that he was dead, I made my way back over to Cotton and Maverick. The Python's numbers were depleting fast. Their casualties were building with every shot we fired, and a wave of satisfaction washed over me when I realized that Styx wasn't alone in his death. By the time we made it over to the warehouse, the area was clear of Pythons.

Maverick turned to Cotton and asked, "You want us to check inside the warehouse?"

"Do a sweep just to be sure," he answered.

We made our way inside, ensuring that no one had been left behind. By the time we returned, everyone had gathered in front of the warehouse, and Rip and Dive were talking to

Cotton.

"It's done. All clear," Maverick told him.

"There's a shitload of artillery they left behind in there," I informed him. "At least twenty-five crates of guns and drugs."

"Get the truck over here. We're taking it with us," Cotton ordered.

"We got 'em, Prez," Boozer told him proudly. "We won the war."

"Not sure about that," Dive corrected him. "Think I saw something, but it was dark. I couldn't be certain."

"What do you think you saw?" Guardrail barked.

"Not sure. It was out of our line of vision. You might want to check the camera feed," Dive told him.

Cotton quickly pulled up the security camera on his phone, searching through everything that had been captured over the past hour. We all watched the blood drained from his face as he stared at the face that crossed the screen.

He turned to us with a look of pure anguish and said, "Fuck! I can't believe I didn't see it. It was right there in black and white, and I just didn't see it. This fight wasn't just about taking over our territory or running drugs through our town. It was more – so much more. We didn't win this fucking war. This battle has just begun."

Chapter 25

WREN

WHEN I GOT to the room, Dusty and Wyatt were dressed in their pajamas and sitting on the bed whispering to each other about something. Their eyes widened when I closed the door behind me and asked, "What are you two up to?"

"Can Wya-it sleep in my room tonight?" Dusty asked with a pleading look. "I've got bunk beds, and he can sleep on top."

"Please, Momma. I don't have school tomorrow, and I've always wanted to sleep on bunk beds."

The entire scene caught me off guard. Wyatt had only stayed the night with my parents and had never really been interested in staying with a friend before. It surprised me that he wanted to spend the night with Dusty tonight, especially after everything that had happened with him today. His little eyes danced with excitement as he waited for my answer. A huge smile crossed his face when I said, "I don't mind. You can go, but I want you to get some rest."

"Awesome!" Dusty shouted happily.

"Don't stay up too late," I insisted. "And if you need me, just call or come back to the room. I'll be here."

"Okay," Wyatt answered as he ran over to me, giving me a quick hug before he headed for the door. I smiled when I heard their laughter bouncing down the hall as they both raced to Dusty's room. It did my heart good to see him so happy, and I truly hoped that Wyatt and Dusty would become good friends. But my smile slowly began to fade when I looked down at the rips and tears on my blood stained clothes. I was a mess and in a desperate need for a hot shower. I went over to the large dresser to hunt for some clean clothes and was surprised to see that everything that I'd packed from home was neatly tucked away inside. I checked each drawer looking for something comfortable to wear, but nothing really called out to me. When I finally opened the last drawer, Griffin's jeans and shirts laid there staring back at me. I couldn't resist. I liked the thought of wearing something of his, so I quickly grabbed one of the soft cotton t-shirts and headed to the bathroom.

After removing my dirty clothes and bandages, I stepped into the hot shower. The cuts on my wrists and hands began to sting as the water flowed down my body, but I didn't move. I needed to feel the burn, using it to pull me from the haze that I'd fallen into since I found myself locked away in that damn trunk. Everything that had happened in the past twenty-four hours had become a blur in my mind. Every face, every word, and every action were meshing together into one horrific moment that I desperately wanted to forget. I just wanted to be back in Griffin's bed, curled up next to him with my head on his chest, listening to the rhythm of his heart beat. Damn, I missed him. I missed the sound of his voice and the touch of his skin against mine. I just wanted him to come back.

When I stepped out of the shower, my muscles felt looser, almost back to normal as I walked over to the mirror above the sink. I took my towel and wiped the fog from the glass, and once it was clear, I was shocked by what I saw. Dark bruises were scattered across my side, looking worse than I had imagined, but thankfully, my ribs weren't hurting like they were a few hours ago. I quickly replaced my bandages and put on Griffin's t-shirt. I was exhausted, so I curled up in the bed, pulling the covers over me. I thought I was feeling better, until the moment I closed my eyes and saw Griffin's face.

I was scared. I tried to convince myself that he was going to be fine, that as the enforcer, he'd been in situations like this before, but it didn't make me feel any better. Until I laid my eyes on him, nothing was going to take away my worry. To some extent, his life would always be filled with danger, and I would have to learn to accept that, learn to live with the worry. I may never know why he'd chosen to do the things he'd done, but the fact remained that he *knew*. He knew that precious lives were at stake, Wyatt's, mine, and his brothers, and I had no doubt that he would do whatever it took to keep us all safe.

I'd been laying there, staring at the ceiling for almost an hour when he stepped into the room. He was quiet, and I could feel the tension rolling off of him as he closed the door behind him. Without turning on the lights, he came over and sat on the edge of bed next to me, and even in the dark, I could see that something was weighing on his mind. He let out a deep breath as he leaned over, resting his elbows on his knees as he stared down at the floor.

"Hey," I whispered, but he didn't turn back to look at me. I sat up and reached for the lamp beside the bed. When the light revealed his blood soaked clothing, I shouted, "Griffin! Are you okay?"

"I'm fine, Wren. Nothing for you to worry about," he said with his eyes still glued to the floor.

"You're bleeding," I cried as I got out of the bed and knelt down in front of him, reaching out for the hem of his shirt. His eyes locked on mine as I pulled it over his head and tossed it on the floor. I winced when I spotted the bullet wound on his arm. "This isn't nothing, Griffin. You've been shot!"

"I'm fine," he grumbled. "Just a graze."

I reached down and he didn't resist when I pulled off his boots. I rested them down on the floor, then took his hand and led him into the bathroom. After turning on the shower, I walked back over to him and silently reached for the buckle of his jeans. When they dropped to the floor, he stood there frozen, watching me intently as he waited to see what I was going to do next. I eased my t-shirt over my head and laid it across the sink. His eyes quickly dropped to the bruises on my side, and his face grew pale.

"Fuck," he growled.

"Don't," I scolded. "It looks worse than it really is." I took his hand and led him into the shower. He stood there silent as the warm water cascaded down his broad shoulders, easing some of the tension that settled in his muscles.

With his eyes closed in anguish, he whispered, "They could've killed you tonight."

I lifted my hands to his face, placing the palms of my hands on his jaw, forcing him to look at me and said, "But they didn't. I'm stronger than you give me credit for."

When he didn't respond, I took the washcloth and lathered it with soap, gently washing away blood that covered his body. He arched his back and placed his hands flat against the shower wall as I ran the cloth along his back.

Without looking at me, he said, "I saw the way you looked at me tonight when you found out that I'd killed Victor. He wasn't the first man I've killed, and he won't be the last."

"I know that," I admitted.

He turned to face me, studying my reaction as he asked, "And you're suddenly okay with that? You don't mind that I've killed men with my bare hands, and I will again to protect my family? Can you really give your heart to me... let your son be around a man like me?"

"Yes," I told him with no hesitation.

"How can you say that?" he growled.

I placed my hands on his chest and said, "You're the club Enforcer. It's your job. It is part of who you are, but there is so much more to you than just that title. I can't understand why you do those things, but the parts that I do understand about you are so strong that they override any doubts that I may have. As for Wyatt, I've already seen the influence you've had on him. And that is a large part of why I love you so. You may be the Enforcer of your club, but you are the protector of Wyatt and me. You give us the stability we've never had. I'll just have to accept that there is a part of your life that I may never understand, but I believe in you enough to be able to focus on what you and I are together. It's good, and I love you."

His eyes searched my face, seeking some kind of confirmation that what I'd said was true. Warm water flowed down around us as I wrapped my arms around his neck, pulling him closer. The shadows of doubt began to fade into the light when I touched him, reassuring him that I'd meant what I had said.

"Griffin, I..." I started, but my words fell silent as he quickly closed the distance between us and took me in his arms. All of the uncertainty on his face immediately melted away as he leaned down and pressed his lips against mine. The minute our mouths touched, I felt an immediate rush of anticipation. There was something intoxicating about his touch, and just being near him made me want to lose control. I wanted to give in to him, give him my heart, my body... everything. Pure lust washed over me as I wrapped my arms around his neck, pulling him closer as I pressed my breasts against his chest.

"Say it again," he groaned as his mouth hovered over my neck, the warmth of his breath tickling against my flesh.

I held him tightly as I whispered, "I love you."

He began nipping and sucking my neck as he said, "I should've walked away, left you alone, but I just couldn't do it. I was powerless to leave you. I had to have you." He lifted his head and looked at me. His eyes pierced through me with an intensity I'd never known as he said, "I had to know what it felt like to be loved by you, and now that I know, there's no way I'll ever be able to let you go."

His lips pressed unrestrained against mine, matching my need for him. A soft moan escaped me as his tongue swept across my lips, compelling them to open. I didn't resist, and his tongue surged into my mouth, winding with mine in a rush of passion that I couldn't refuse. His arms wrapped around my body, and carefully lifted me from the floor as he eased my back against the shower wall. He was trying not to hurt me, avoiding the bruises that marked my skin, but I didn't need him to be careful. My mind wasn't focused on the pain at my side. It was all honed in on him and the way he made me feel. The warm water trickled down between our bodies as I began to kiss and suck along his neck, tasting the mingled flavors of his skin and the water.

Goosebumps prickled across my flesh as the bristles of his beard raked across my bare skin. Wanting more, my head fell back, exposing the curves of my neck. His eyes sparkled with lust as he watched the droplets of water gliding down my breasts. Slowly, he moved his mouth down my slick skin, slowly brushing his fingers against my breasts as he made his way down to my hip. I groaned in pleasure as his hand found its way between my legs. The tips of his fingers glided over my wet clit, making my knees buckle beneath me. My body began to tremble, forcing me to shift my leg to the side as he thrust two fingers deep inside me. I shamelessly bucked my hips forward as I rocked against his hand.

"I don't think I'll ever get enough of you," he whispered as he dropped to his knees, settling between my legs. He slowly ran his tongue across my clit as he continued to curl his fingers deep inside of me. I reached down, letting my fingers tangle into his hair as he tormented me with his tongue.

I loved the feeling of his warm, wet mouth against me, and back arched as I cried out in ecstasy, "Griffin! Oh God, I'm coming.... Don't stop!"

He wrapped his mouth around my clit, pressing his tongue firmly against it as he moved his fingers inside me. My hips jolted against him while he continued to torture me with his mouth, my body clenching firmly around his fingers as I came. He slowly began to stand while he moved his fingers back and forth inside me, my entire body tensing with my release. Once he had removed his fingers, he placed his hands on my hips, turning me around to face the shower wall. I rested the palms of my hands against the wet tile as his hard cock pressed against me.

"You want my cock?" he taunted.

"Um..hmm." I answered.

"Tell me, Wren. Tell me that you want my cock, that you love me and want me inside you."

"I want you, Griffin. I want you, now," I whimpered. As soon as he slid his cock deep inside me, I said, "I love you."

His fingers dug into my flesh as he held onto my hip as he pulled back and drove inside me again. I braced my hands against the tile as I let my body adjust to the rhythm of his movements.

"I love you," I whimpered over and over again as he drove into me harder with each and every thrust, our bodies slamming into each other. He felt so good inside me, driving me wild with a passion I'd never known. I couldn't restrain myself, and began rocking back against him, meeting each and every thrust. His hand reached for my hair, pulling my head back towards him so he could kiss and suck along my neck.

"You're mine. Now and forever," he growled as his rhythm increased. As the need to climax began to overtake me, my body began to spasm around him, signaling him that I was about to lose control. With his free hand, he reached around me, pressing firmly as he circled his fingers around my clit. I tilted my ass towards him, grinding harder against his cock as he drove deeper inside me. My body began to tremble as my orgasm took hold, my muscles contracting around him and pulling him deeper inside me. His growl echoed around us as his entire body tensed and he came inside me.

"Fuck!" he roared as his fingers dug into my hips, holding me firmly in place. After several seconds, his breathing began to slow and he released me, just long enough to turn me around to face him. He placed his hands on my face, forcing me to look at him when he said, "I've never known love like this, never felt it, never even knew I wanted it. But I want it now, and nothing is going to stop me from having it. I love you, Wren."

Chapter 26

STITCH

WREN'S FACE TWISTED into a worried frown as she checked my wound and said, "I think you may need stitches."

"It'll be fine," I assured her.

"It's not fine. You need to let Doc take a look at it," she scolded.

"You're looking at it. Don't need Doc," I provoked as I dropped my towel to the floor and reached for my sweats, slowly pulling them over my hips as Wren watched intently. Her face flushed red with desire when her eyes dropped, roaming slowly over my body. I loved the way she looked at my body, like she'd never be able to get enough of me. I stared at her standing there in my t-shirt, looking sexy as fuck, and she completely captivated me. I found myself want-ing to take her all over again.

Sensing my thoughts, she took a step back and said, "Don't even think about it, mister. I'm going to bandage your arm before there is any more of that."

"Come here," I commanded.

"Griffin," she warned.

"*Wren*," I said firmly as I leaned against the dresser. My lips immediately curled into a smile when she stepped closer, settling between my legs. She placed the palms of her hands on my chest, looking up at me with anticipation. When I didn't move, she gave me a puzzled look. I placed my hand under her chin and said, "You need to know that you're it for me, Wren. I'm claiming you as mine."

"Claiming me?"

"Yes. I want everyone to know you are mine," I explained.

Her hands slipped around my neck as she smiled and said, "So, you want me to be your old lady?"

"For now. But when things settle down with the club, I'm going to put a ring on your finger, make you mine in every way."

"I like the sound of that," she answered before pressing her lips to mine. With just a simple touch, the kiss became heated, full of need and want. I couldn't get enough of her. I reached for the hem of her t-shirt, but quickly stopped when there was a knock on the door.

"Momma?" Wyatt cried. As Wren quickly turned and headed for the door, I reached for a clean shirt.

When she opened the door, she knelt down in front of him and asked, "Hey, Buddy. What's wrong?"

"This cast is bothering me. I want to take this stupid thing off. I can't sleep with it on. I keep bumping it on the rails of the bed and the wall," Wyatt pouted. "And it's starting to itch a little."

"Sorry, honey, but you're pretty much stuck with it for the next few weeks," she explained.

He let out a disgruntled sigh and said, "Okay."

"You want to sleep in here with me?" Wren asked him.

"No. I'm going back to Dusty's room. His bunk beds are cool, and he's letting me sleep on top," he answered. Just before he turned to leave, he looked over to me and asked, "Hey, Griffin. Will you sign my cast tomorrow?"

"You know I will. I'm sure some of the other guys will want to sign it, too," I told him.

His eyes lit up with excitement when he said, "That'd be awesome." He paused for a minute, then asked, "What about your president? You think he'd sign it?"

"Yeah. He'll sign it for ya."

"That would be so cool. The president of Satan's Fury... Thomas never had anything like that," he said excitedly as he stepped forward and gave Wren a quick hug. "I better get back before

Dusty wakes up and sees that I'm gone."

"Okay. I'm here if you need anything," she told him as she watched him take off down the hall. When she knew that he was in Dusty's room, she closed the door and headed over to the bed. She down on the edge of the bed and asked, "So, what's the story with Dusty? He is such a cute kid, and Wyatt seems to really like him."

"Awesome kid. He's had a rough go of it, but you'd never know it. He lost his dad a few months back, and it was pretty hard on him," I explained.

"I can't imagine how hard that must have been on him and his poor mother," she whispered with an anguished look.

"It hasn't been easy on any of them, but they're finding their way. I think Dusty has been a real comfort to his mother."

"She's lucky to have him. He seems like a sweet child," she smiled. "He's definitely made an impression on Wyatt."

"He's made an impression on all of us."

With a silent yawn, she laid back in the bed and said, "I guess you have that in common with him, then. You tend to make a lasting impression on people, too."

"Is that right?" I asked her as I turned off the light and settled in the bed next to her.

She nestled into my side, resting her head on

my chest and said, "Yep. Very impressionable."

"Get some sleep," I laughed.

"I love you," she whispered and the room fell silent as she quickly drifted off to sleep.

I looked down at her, watching the rise and fall of her chest as she slept. She was perfect, more than I ever dared to dream for, and she was mine. I loved the feel of her body close to mine, and I wanted this moment with her to last, but I could barely keep my eyes open. I reluctantly I closed them, finally giving in to my own exhaustion. Hours later, my phone started ringing. When it started ringing for the second time, I reluctantly got up, cursing under my breath, and answered the call.

Before I even had a chance to speak, Guardrail said, "Cotton's called us into church. Be there in ten." Then the phone line went dead.

I quickly got dressed, and as I headed for the door, I looked over to Wren curled up in the covers. She was still sleeping soundly, completely content lying there in my bed, and I wanted nothing more than to crawl back into the bed next to her. Unable to stop myself, I walked over to her and kissed her lightly on the forehead. Her eyes fluttered open, and I pressed my lips against hers once more and said, "I've gotta go for a bit. Cotton has called us in, but I'll be back as soon as I can."

"Okay," she answered sleepily.

"Try to go back to sleep," I told her as closed the door behind me and headed to church. When I walked into the room, Cotton was already sitting down at the front of the table, and my brothers were quickly following suit.

Once we were all seated, Cotton said, "It was Derek. He was the man who we caught on the security feed." The room fell silent as we all tried to comprehend what he'd just said. I'd heard about Derek in random conversations, but never thought much about him. He was before my time, long before I ever joined the club.

"Your cousin?" Guardrail asked, running his hand through his hair in aggravation.

"Yeah, that's him. Until last night, I hadn't seen him in almost twenty years," Cotton explained.

"So why do you think he's back now?" Maverick asked.

"Vengeance... an ultimate, horrific kind of vengeance." He paused, letting out a deep breath, then said, "We were close once, but when we got older, things changed. Derek was different... there was an evil about him that set everyone on edge."

He looked down at the table as he took a moment to collect his thoughts. Then, he continued, "Even though he loved Derek, my uncle knew that he could never take his place as President. It was then that he took me under his wing.

When the time came for him to step down, he named me as his predecessor. Derek stood there, listening to the news and it just broke something inside of him. He was never the same after that."

"It was the right decision," Doc interrupted. "That boy was a loose cannon. Always getting into shit. None of us wanted him taking over the club."

"Maybe so, but Derek didn't see it that way. He tried to stick it out with the club, but jealousy got the best of him. Never could get past thinking that I had taken what was his. I can still remember the night he came into my room with that fucking knife. Stuck the damn thing to my throat while I was sleeping. We both knew he could have killed me, but he just fucking laughed in my face. That night he promised that he'd be back, and he would do whatever it took to destroy me. I'm not a man that gets shaken easily, but the way he looked at me, the hatred in his voice... it got me," he explained.

"So this is a vendetta?" I asked.

"Absolutely. Actually surprised it's taken him this long to come back," Cotton replied. "When I saw him on that screen, I knew this wasn't over. He didn't have the look of a man that felt threatened by us, worried that we were about to take him down. It was just the opposite. He stood there gloating, knowing that we were playing right into his fucking hands."

"What are you planning to do now?" I asked, knowing that he wasn't going to let anything happen to his club. He'd worked too hard to let this motherfucker come in and take it all away.

"This is about him wanting to get to me. Make me pay for what I took from him. I'm not going to let that happen... we're not going to let that happen," Cotton declared. It was obvious that the news he'd shared was taking its toll on him, and we all wondered just exactly how he planned to handle it. Whatever he decided, we would have his back. When things in my life hit rock bottom, Cotton was there, and he'd been there, standing by me ever since. It was that way with all of us. Cotton never failed to be there for his brothers, and it was our time to be there for him. "For now, we stay on lockdown. Keep our families close, and I'm going to make contact with Derek. In the meantime, I think it's time to have a vote on Two Bit and Q'. They've proved themselves loyal and true to the club, and it's time to patch them in," Cotton explained. "All in favor of Two Bit being patched in say aye."

"Aye," we all answered.

"Q'?"

The room was filled with another unanimous, "Aye."

"The vote has been made. Two Bit and Q' will be patched into the club. Tonight we'll celebrate and put all this shit with Derek on hold while we show our new brothers some heartfelt gratitude," he ordered. With that, he slammed his gavel on the table and stood to leave.

Chapter 27

WREN

"**S**O, IT'S OFFICIAL," Henley smiled. "You're an old lady."

"Never thought I'd be happy to be called that," I laughed.

Emerson leaned forward and smiled as she teased, "You sure you're up for this? He can be pretty bossy."

"I think I can handle it," I laughed.

"I never thought I'd see him so happy. I'm so glad that he found you," Emerson explained.

"I think this calls for a celebration," Cassidy announced. "Who's up for a round of shots?"

"Ah… you and the damn shots. Are you trying to kill me?" Henley whined.

"I didn't say you had to drink ten of them," Cassidy scolded.

"I totally blame you for letting me get carried away the other night. You're supposed to watch out for your little sister," Henley feigned a pout.

"Yeah, well, that's a full time job, kiddo," Cassidy laughed.

"I'll have one," Allie answered as she looked behind her, checking to see if her husband was still playing pool. "Maybe two if Guardrail's game doesn't end soon."

Cassidy reached behind the bar and pulled out the bottle of tequila, placing it on the counter next to the salt and limes. Henley took the shot glass in her hand and tilted her head back, quickly swallowing it as she reached for a lime. When she was done, she sat the glass on the counter and said, "I heard Maverick telling some of the guys that you got out of a trunk all by yourself. Kicked your way out! Girl, color me impressed."

"There's nothing like the drive of a mother's determination," I laughed. Then I took my drink and said, "I'm just having one. Dallas is watching the boys, and I told her I'd be back early to put Wyatt to bed."

"It's been good to see Dallas again. She seems to be doing better. Losing Skidrow hit her hard, but she's finally getting back on her feet," Henley explained.

"I think knowing Victor has been taken care of helped her with that," Cassidy mumbled under her breath.

"Victor?" I asked.

"Victor is the guy that killed Skid," Cassidy answered. I knew the name Victor. I don't think

I will ever forget it. My thoughts instantly drifted back to my conversation with Doc. I remembered him telling me that Stitch did whatever it took to protect his brothers, and I knew then exactly what he'd meant. Before I had a chance to question her further, she quickly changed the subject by saying, "How does Wyatt like the clubhouse?"

"He loves it," I answered.

"Wyatt is too cute for words," Allie told me. "When I mentioned that I had a German Shepherd, he told me everything about the breed and how important it was to train them properly. Even told me how to get him to stop chewing on the legs of my furniture."

"I'm sure he did! He's been begging me for a dog for months. He researched every breed from Shih Tzu's to Great Danes," I explained. "When he sets his mind to something, it's hard to get him to think about anything else."

"Well, you should definitely bring him by to meet Charlie sometime," Allie offered. "He's really friendly, and I'm sure that Wyatt would love him."

"I'd love to bring him by. I'm sure he'd love that," I told her.

"I'll get Guardrail to grill out for us. You girls should come, too. Bring the guys," Allie told them.

"I'd love that," Henley answered.

We spent the next hour talking, and I really enjoyed getting to know each of them a little better. Tonight was the first time I'd gotten to spend any time with Allie, but I could tell that we had a lot in common. I looked forward to getting to know her even better. Cassidy poured us each another shot, but her expression immediately changed when Cotton came in and sat down at the end of the bar. Tension washed over her as she glanced over at him, and I couldn't help but wonder what was bothering her.

When she let out a deep sigh, I whispered, "Are you okay?"

She forced a fake smile and said, "Absolutely. Never been better. Just need..."

"Cass," Cotton called, interrupting her.

With an overstated eye roll, Cassidy answered, "Yeah?"

"Need a beer."

"And?" she asked, placing her hand on her hip.

His eyebrows furrowed in anger when he said, "*Cass.*"

She hesitated, but gave in and walked over to him, handing him a beer from the cooler. I couldn't hear what he was saying to her, but it was clear that he wasn't happy with her. With an irritated scowl, he leaned closer to her, talking to her in a disapproving tone. When he was done scolding her, she turned her back to him and started to walk out of the bar. She was clearly angry, but he quickly reached out and grabbed her arm, pulling her close to his chest. He said something else to her, but when she snapped back at him, he instantly stood and with his hand still wrapped around her elbow, he led her out of the bar.

"It's about damn time," Henley said smiling.

"I'm lost. How is what just happened a good thing?" I asked.

Henley let out a deep breath and said, "There's always been a push and pull with those two. I've never really understood it, but it's worked for them. But lately, for whatever reason, Cotton has been trying to keep his distance from Cassidy, and she hasn't been handling it very well. Actually, it's made her bat-shit crazy. Maybe now they will either end this thing between them once and for all, or get their shit together."

"What do you think they'll do?" I asked.

"There's no telling," Henley said. "But I know Cassidy, and if there's something she wants, she isn't going to let it go without a fight."

Chapter 28

STITCH

A year later

"**C**AN I HAVE mine plain?" Wyatt asked anxiously. "I don't like ketchup. Tomatoes are gross."

We were in the kitchen, and Wyatt was watching as I put the seasoning on the burger meat. I'd managed to convince him that I made better burgers than the ones that they made down at the diner, but I could see that he was having his doubts. "Yeah, you can have yours plain."

"What else are we having?"

"Haven't really thought about it. Whatcha got in mind?" I asked.

"Mom usually makes something healthy," he said with his nose crinkling with dislike.

"We could do fries or chips? What do you think about that?"

"Yeah, I like French fries, but I like them

plain. No ketchup," he reminded me.

"You got it," I told him. "You want to help me start up the grill?"

"Yes! Can I light it?" he asked. "I'll be real careful."

"Yeah, you can light it, but we'll need to get the charcoal set up first," I told him as I started towards the back porch. Once we were outside, I handed him the large bag of charcoal and guided him over to the grill. "You'll need to pour it out slow, so they don't get away from you. Then, we've got to stack them up kinda like a pyramid."

"I can do that," he said proudly as he lifted the bag, pouring the charcoal out onto the grate. Once he emptied the bag, he reached in and started to organize each of the little squares, trying to create a perfect pyramid. It took some time, but I let him get it done the way he wanted before I handed him the barbeque lighter. He pushed the button several times before it finally lit, then he eased it down to the charcoal, smiling wide when the fire took hold. "I did it," he said proudly.

"Yep. You did good, Bud."

"Can I help you cook the burgers, too?" he asked, flicking his wrists at his sides as he lifted up on his tiptoes.

"Absolutely," I smiled. When we walked back into the kitchen, Wren was leaning into the refrigerator looking for something to munch on, and Wyatt wasted no time letting her know what he'd been up to. "I got to light the grill, and Griff said I could help make the burgers!"

"That's awesome. Do you need any help? I could make a salad," she offered.

"We've got this," I told her, kissing her lightly on the lips as I eased her to the side and closed the refrigerator. She placed her hands on her very round belly and gave me a small pout. "Let the men tend to their business."

"Yeah, Mom. We've got this," Wyatt mocked.

"Well, I'll just leave my boys to it then," she smiled and waddled towards the living room.

Wyatt followed me back out to the porch and listened intently as I showed him how to grill the burgers. While the meat sizzled under the heat of the fire, we both sat quietly in our rocking chairs lost in our own thoughts. I looked over to him and couldn't believe how surreal it all felt. There was a time when I never would have dreamed that my life could turn out like this. I was scared to even imagine that I could have a family and a life that I actually enjoyed living. I'd spent so much time just trying to survive, never thinking that I would have people in my life that actually cared about me, much less a pregnant wife and a son that I adored. My life was good.

"I think they're ready," Wyatt said, pulling me from my thoughts.

"Let's get them off then," I told him and headed for the grill. Excitement rolled off him as he used the spatula to take the meat off all by himself. When he was done, he proudly took the tray of burgers and placed it on the table. Then, he raced over to the counter to get our drinks, while I brought the fries over. Once everything was set, he shouted, "Mom!! It's ready!"

"Griffin, can you come here a minute," she called.

I stuck my head into the living room and found her standing there with her hands cradling her stomach while she stared down at the floor. I took a step forward, quickly noticing the pool of water at her feet. "Wren? What's going on?"

She looked up at me and tried to remain calm as she said, "My water just broke."

"Your water did what?" I was prepared for this moment. Did everything I could think of to make sure I knew what to expect, but the minute I realized she was in labor, my mind drew a blank.

"It just means the amniotic sac broke, re-member? We read about it in that book Mom gave you. She's in labor," Wyatt interrupted. "The baby is coming. Right, Momma?"

"That's right, buddy. In a few hours, you'll get to meet your new sister," she explained. How the hell could she be standing there seeming so fucking composed? The woman was in labor, the baby was coming, and she was standing there talking all calm and shit like there was nothing to it. I'd always been the one that was in control, prepared for anything, but at that moment, I felt like someone had stripped me of all my power, and I was helpless to do anything about it.

"Oh… and we need to call your grandparents and tell them to meet us at the hospital," Wren explained.

"I'll do it," Wyatt told her as he headed to get his phone. Just before he left the room, he looked over to me and said, "Don't forget to go get Momma's bag and put it in the car."

"Where's the bag? Did you get everything packed?" I asked with panic.

Wren looked at me and with a soft voice said, "Come here."

When I walked over to her, she placed her hands on my face and said, "In a few hours, you are going to be a daddy. You're going to hold your precious, little girl in your arms, and the wait will be over. We'll finally get to meet our daughter. I need you to take a deep breath and help me change out of these wet clothes, so we can go to the hospital."

"And the bag?"

"Honey, you put it in the car days ago. Remember?" she teased.

"I did?"

When she nodded, I took her hand and

helped her to the bedroom. As soon as she was changed, we all headed to the car. Even though I was a nervous wreck, Wren remained calm the entire way to the hospital. Wyatt sat in the backseat, spouting off facts about the delivery that I *really* didn't need to hear. Wren rested her hand on my shoulder and whispered, *"Breathe."*

After hours of watching Wren struggle through the pains of labor, our beautiful daughter was born. With Wyatt standing by my side, I held my Mia close to my chest, looking at her with complete awe. I felt as if my heart might burst inside my chest as I stared down at her. She had a full head of brown hair and little blue eyes like her brother. She was perfect, just like her mother had promised.

"It just keeps getting better. How is that possible?" I asked Wren.

"I don't know, but it's just going to keep getting better," Wren whispered. *"Trust me."*

Acknowledgements

Followed by a short excerpt of Maverick

I am extremely blessed to have such an incredible mother. Every day, she is there supporting me and encouraging me to be the best that I can be. I wouldn't know what to do without her. Thank you, Mom. You make my life better just by being in it.

I would also like to give a huge thank you to my PA, Amanda Faulkner. She's truly unbelievable! Posts, teasers, blogs…. It never ends. Thank you so much, Amanda!! Your help means the world to me. If you are in the need of a great PA or a great blog to follow, be sure to check out her links located under the title page.

Marci Ponce, you are an amazing editor and friend. Not only do you listen to me vent when my life gets hectic, (and I get down in the swamps) you still manage to keep me on track with my writing. I truly wouldn't know what to do without you. You push me to be the best I can be and accept nothing less with each and every book. Your entire family has shown true dedication to the series, and it has meant so very much to me. Thank you so much for always being there and sharing your talent with me. I love ya, chick!

Danielle Deraney Palumbo, you've done it again! Even though your life has been extremely hectic, you still took the time to give me feedback on Stitch and help make it even better. I can't tell you how much your help has meant to me. Thank you so much for everything you do, including kind words of support. You are amazing!

I would also like to thank all of my readers. I have loved all of your comments and posts. It means so much to me to hear that you have enjoyed reading one of my books. You have all been so supportive, and your comments always leave a smile on my face. When my life gets a little crazy, your kind words have given me the encouragement I've needed to continue on. Thank you Leah Joslin for being there to make me smile and encourage me when things get hectic. It has meant such much to me. You rock!

My Wilder's Women Street Rocks!!! Thank you all for your support. It means so much to me that you continue to help me with reviews and posting all of my teasers. Elizabeth Thiele, Neringa Neringiukas, Dawn Bryant, Mary Orr, Tanya Skaggs, and Rosetta Wagers are such a huge help to me. I am always amazed each time I see one of my teasers or my links that they have shared. Thank you for taking your time to help me. It means more than you will ever know.

I have been very blessed to have so much support from such a great group of women. Sue

Banner, Tanya Skaggs, Patricia Ann Blevins, Sherri Crowder, RB Hilliard, Keeana Porter, Terra Oenning, Danielle Palumbo, Kimberely Beale, Michelle Modesitte, Stacie Page – Ramay, Dana Kimberely Wade, Race Crespin, and Brandy Kennedy, you guys never fail to make me smile with your amazing reviews and kind words! Thanks so much for taking the time to read my books. Your reviews and comments mean so much to me!

Another special thank you to Sue Banner. From the start, she has shown me so much kindness and it has meant so much to me. She takes time out of her busy schedule to help make sure the book is ready for you, and she does an amazing job. She also helps edit her son's book. If you haven't had a chance to check out Daryl Banner's books, you are missing out.

facebook.com/DarylBannerWriter

http://tinyurl.com/pzogl4p

Ana Rosso, my little grasshopper, thank you for always being there to read all the various editions of my books, making sure that I get it just right. Even though you are hundreds of miles away, you are like my personal cheerleader. I hope to do the same for you when your new book releases! Can't wait! Keep on rocking chickeroo!!

MAVERICK

Excerpt from Book 1 in the Satan's Fury MC Series

My mother used to say that everything happens for a reason. It didn't matter how insignificant or how heart-wrenchingly tragic, she'd say it was just meant to be. She truly believed that if a person was patient enough... looked hard enough... for *long* enough, they'd be able to find their silver lining. Her faith never faltered. Facing difficult times with strength and determination, my loving mother would wait... no matter how long it took. It might have taken her months or even years, but my mother would always be able to find that light shining at the end of the long, dark tunnel.

I say bullshit. There is *no fucking silver lining*. Shit happens. Hard times are just a part of life, like the air we breathe. We have to learn to deal with the hand we are dealt and move the hell on. Yet, every damn time something fucked up happens in my life, I find myself thinking of my mother. If she were still alive, I wonder what she'd have to say about everything that's happened in my life over the last year. Would she be able to find my silver lining? Because, I sure as hell can't.

Chapter 1

MAVERICK

"**D**ON'T RUSH INTO this, Maverick. I know what you're like. Give it some time, brother," Cotton told me. I could see the concern in his penetrating eyes, and it meant a lot to me that he was trying to help. He was a good man... a good President. The brothers of Satan's Fury looked up to him-admired him. We all knew that the club was his life, and he was all about the brotherhood. As our President, he had no problem sacrificing everything for the club – even laying down his own life, time and time again, if it meant protecting his family. I respected him for that, and was honored to be a part of it. "I know what's really going on here. You can blame this on whatever you want, but the truth is glaring you right in the face."

"He's my son! What kind of man would I be if I put him in danger? I can't risk it, Cotton," I told him, as I looked down at my broken arm that was now wrapped up in a sling. I was a fucking mess. Bruises and cuts covered my body from head to toe. They'd done a pretty good job of working me over, and I still couldn't figure out why they didn't just kill me when they had the chance. "Think about it. What if he was with me when those motherfuckers jumped me? It's up to me to protect him, and I couldn't live with myself if something happened to him. I already ruined his mother's life, and I'll be damned if I ruin his."

"That's bullshit, and you know it. Hailey brought that shit on herself. You can't keep carrying all of the blame," Cotton snapped.

"It was my fault! All if it! I wasn't there when she needed me. I should have stuck with her, made sure she got the help she needed. Now she's dead, and I have to own that. John Warren is all I have left of her. I can't let anything happen to him."

"Nothing's going to happen to him, Maverick," he assured me, but we both knew he couldn't guarantee that. "None of that even matters... it's all in the past. Right now, you have to face your demons, either fight them or learn to live with them."

I knew he was right. My mind had been a cluster fuck since the day I brought John Warren home with me. When I looked at him, I could tell that he had my blood running through his veins. He was such a good looking kid – healthy and strong. I was thankful that his mother's drug use hadn't hurt him. Yet, there was a question lingering deep inside of me. I couldn't put my finger on it. Why did this strange pull keep going off in my head? I loved this kid from the start, but my mind was bombarded with doubts – some of which I couldn't even name. I had to believe that I was doing this for him. I'd fucked up so much already, I couldn't be responsible for ruining another life. Me... the club... whatever the reason, John Warren didn't belong here with me. He deserved more.

"I can't take that chance. I can't make the same mistakes again, Cotton." My throat tightened, making it difficult to even say the words. I truly believed that taking him to Lily was the right thing to do. He deserved a mother, and I knew she loved him as her own. But, the selfish side of me wished things could be different. Still, I knew I had to protect him at all costs. That was the most important thing now.

"Maverick..." Cotton tried again.

"I need you to back me up on this," I argued. "It's the right thing for John Warren... and for me."

His face was registered with acceptance as he brought his hand up, and rested it on my shoulder. "I wish you'd give it more time, but if this is what you think you should do, I'll support you on it. When do you need to leave?"

I stood up and reached for my keys. "Tonight. There's no need in delaying this thing any longer. It's a long drive, so it will take me a couple of days to get back."

"I'll let the guys know. Just be careful," Cotton told me as I turned towards the door. "Maverick?"

I looked over towards him as Cotton said, "Some choices can't be undone. You need to be sure about this one, brother." My eyes dropped down to the floor. The worn out boards creaked beneath my feet, and I wondered how they managed to support my weight. I felt so heavy, like the unrelenting weight of the world was pressing down on my shoulders. It hurt to move... to even breathe. His words circled through my thoughts, and I knew he was right. This one decision could haunt me for the rest of my life, but I knew in my gut it was the right thing to do for John Warren... for my son.

I opened the door to my room, and stopped. It was hard to believe how much this room had changed in just one week. It'd been just a room. A place to crash when I needed it, but now I didn't recognize it. John Warren's presence filled the air, surrounding me with his warmth. My chest tightened as I thought about him not being here anymore. I tried to block the turmoil from my mind as I grabbed a bag and quickly began filling it with his clothes and toys. When I picked up the tiny giraffe that he slept with every night, I couldn't hold it together any longer. My legs began to buckle under me when I thought about him lying in that crib with his tiny little fingers wrapped around the giraffe's neck. It gutted me. I dropped down to my knees as I held the stuffed animal tightly in my hands, bringing it up close to my face so I could inhale JW's scent. Damn. I'd never felt a hurt like this before.

Why did it have to be like this? Why couldn't I be the father he needed? What the fuck was wrong with me? My chest tightened when I thought about taking him back to Lily. My heart shattered like broken glass when I thought about not being able to see his smile; to touch him... to hold him. He was a part of me – the best part of me – but I couldn't stop the doubts from spiraling through my head. The darkness inside of me was growing, engulfing me. John Warren deserved more than I could give... a life not tarnished by the likes of me.

There was a tap on my door, and I had just enough time to get back on my feet before Cassidy walked in. John Warren was propped up on her hip with a handful of her hair in one hand and a bottle in the other. "I just finished giving little man his dinner and a bath. He's all ready for bed."

"Thanks, Cass." She was one of the bartenders at the club. Even though she sometimes partied with the club girls, I trusted her to watch him. She'd come to love the kid in the short time he'd been here and enjoyed spending time with him. From the moment I brought him into the club, she couldn't get enough of him, always wanting to hold him and play with him. Cass adored him, and I honestly wouldn't have known what to do without her.

I rubbed my eyes with the palm of my hands, trying to clear the tears away. When she noticed the expression on my face, she asked, "What's going on? Are you ok?"

"Would you believe me if I said yes?" I responded, as I looked away from her and started to put the last of John Warren's things in his bag.

"Seriously," she snapped. "Tell me what's going on, Maverick? Are you taking him somewhere?"

I took a deep breath and swallowed hard, trying to reign in the emotions that threatened to tear me apart. I had to hold it together. "I'm taking him back to Lily and Goliath. They can give him what he needs... the life that he deserves..."

"What? No! You can't do that, Maverick... He belongs here, with us... with *you*. You're his dad. You're all he needs," Cassidy cried as the tears began to pool in her eyes.

"Look at him, Cassidy. He's perfect. So innocent… so pure. All the good in the world is wrapped up in him." She looked down at him, a grief-stricken expression on her beautiful face. "I'm no good for him. I'll only fuck it all up if I keep him here. I love him. I love him like nothing else, and I have to protect him… protect him from my world… protect him from *me*." I could feel the storm of emotions begin to take hold again, so I took JW from her arms and picked up his bag. "I don't expect you to understand it, Cassidy, but this is something I have to do. I have to do this for him."

"Please… please don't do this," she begged as she grabbed my arm. Her eyes pleaded with me to listen as she said, "This is a mistake. You're going to regret this for the rest of your life!" I couldn't listen to anymore. Trying my best to block out her cries, I walked past her and out the door.

I was relieved to see that the parking lot was empty as I sat John Warren into his car seat. When I clicked his seatbelt around him, he reached for my hand and smiled. That smile would be forever burned into my mind. I took his little hand and brought it up to my mouth, gently kissing the fingers that wrapped around mine. "I love you, JW. Always will."

I handed the little guy his giraffe as I put the rest of the bags in the seat beside him. I closed his door and got into the car. I sat there for a few minutes in the silence, trying to pull my shit together. Everything was so quiet. It was like I was stuck in some kind of nightmare, lost in a deep fog, and then JW started to babble. He was talking to me like I knew exactly what he was saying.

I turned back to him and said, "I know, little buddy. I know."

I wiped the tears from my eyes and started the engine. It didn't take him long to fall asleep, leaving me with a whirlwind of thoughts and questions. I still couldn't believe how much had happened over the past year. If I had just known... if I hadn't been so stupid and realized everything that was really going on with Hailey, maybe things could have been different.

I'll never forget the first time I laid eyes on her. I'd pulled my bike into an old diner out on Highway 19. It was an out of the way spot, but it was raining, and I was wet and cold. The moment I saw her walk across the floor, I wasn't cold anymore. She was waiting tables, and I wondered why a sexy woman like her was working at a place like this in the middle of nowhere. She had a figure that made a man want to peel her clothes right off, and I would've done just about anything to do just that. I instantly craved the touch of her skin against mine. Her long black hair was pulled back into a ponytail showing off the most beautiful blue eyes I'd ever seen.

Her smile though, that mouth, those lips… damn, she was *perfect*.

One date was all it took. After that, the months rolled by so fast that I lost track of time. It was a whirlwind. She was everything I ever thought I wanted and more. She liked being on the back of my bike and enjoyed hanging with my brothers at the clubhouse. We spent hours talking and drinking with them. She fit. I loved that. We were happy. We'd even started talking about our future, making plans for our life together. She had enrolled in a nursing program and worked every day at the diner to pay for her tuition. Life was good.

Then the nightmare hit. Everything went up in smoke. It was hell. A stupid drunk crashed into Hailey's car, leaving her severely wounded. The dashboard crushed in on her, breaking her leg and fracturing several vertebrae in her neck. It was my fault. I was being selfish that night. I just wanted to be with her every second, and I didn't listen when she told me she was too tired to come to the club. She'd been working all day and just wanted to go home. I should have listened to her, but I was too selfish. I'd had a long day and just wanted inside her.

That crash stole her spark and replaced it with pain and anguish. Her injuries were so painful that the doctors prescribed her strong pain medication, and it seemed to help, giving her some relief from her misery. After she'd been home for a while, I noticed that she was taking too many pills. I figured she was just hurting, and since she was going to school to be a nurse, I thought that she knew what she was doing. A month later, when I saw her taking three at a time, I confronted her about it. She became defensive, but finally admitted that she might have a problem. As time went on, I tried to get her help, sending her to rehab and trying to find doctors that could stop the pain. But nothing worked. The pull of her addiction was already too strong. She tried to hide it from me, over and over again. Each time I discovered that she was still using, she'd promise to try harder. She'd swear that she loved me, and would do whatever it took to get better. I believed her, until the day I found *another* hidden stash of pills. That day, I knew I was done. She chose the drugs over the life we shared, and I refused to be a part of it.

The day I walked out of her life, I prayed that she would straighten herself out and find her way back to me. Instead, she became more and more determined to get her hands on her next fix. When her desperation took hold, she decided to give information about our club in exchange for more drugs. Her betrayal to the club was a decision we'd both come to regret. I should have known that if she would do something like that, she was way past just being in trouble... her life was in true jeopardy. I should've seen she was still struggling, and tried harder to help her. But in truth, it was too late... her lies would send her to her grave. All of her damn lies.

She disappeared for months. No one knew where she was. The club never lets a betrayal go. They searched for her and finally found out that she had been living in a small town just outside of Washington. It looked like she was finally getting her shit together. She'd gotten a job and had a nice place to live. She'd even had a baby. Her neighbor said Hailey was really trying, but it all fell apart. It was just too much for her, and she ended up taking the baby to her mother. My brothers found her dead in her apartment from a drug overdose. It was obvious that it was no accident. Her death hit me hard. I couldn't help but blame myself for what had happened, and the guilt of her death was crippling. But it was nothing compared to the hurt that I felt when I discovered the mountain of secrets she had kept hidden from me.

It was several months after her death when I got an unexpected phone call from a hospital in Paris, Tennessee. A nurse called to tell me that my son had just been in an accident. *My* son. I felt like someone had knocked the wind out of me when I heard those words. My name was listed on his birth certificate, right under Hailey's. It was right there in black and white. I never dreamed the kid that she'd had was mine, and now I had missed almost a year of his life, because Hailey never told me about him. Instead, she took our son to her mother, asking her to protect him from me. Trying to keep her promise, Hailey's mother sent John Warren away. She decided that Lily was the only one that could keep him safe from me and my club. Lily packed him up, and took off for Tennessee. I would have never even known about my son if it hadn't been for his accident. Her mother prayed that I would never find out. She blamed me for Hailey's death. In truth, she was right. Hailey would still be alive if she hadn't been with me. I will never forgive myself for what happened. I had failed her then, but I wouldn't fail her again. I wouldn't let anything happen to our son. I would make sure that he had the life that I couldn't give his mother.

I could barely keep my eyes open by the time I pulled into Lily's driveway. It was Christmas Eve, and the house was lit up with lights, making what I was about to do feel even more impossible. I tried to shake it off. This wasn't about me. It was about John Warren. Giving him a life like this... filled with Christmas trees and family. The life I'd never be able to give him.

Goliath lived the club life, and although his club was different, *safer*, he understood the danger that came along with it. He would know better than anyone why I had to do this. As VP of the Devil Chaser's, he'd seen the hard times of living in a one percenters' club... the uncertainty... the danger. They had put that all behind them, and his club had worked hard to become a legitimate club that was focused on the brotherhood and their families. It was one of the things that I respected most about these men. Nothing was more important than keeping their families safe. I put the car in park, and by the time I turned off the engine and opened the car door, Lily was standing on the front porch.

"What happened to you? Are you ok?" she asked. Her eyes filled with fright as she studied my cuts and bruises. I knew I looked like hell, but I had no intention of telling her what had happened. When I didn't answer, she asked, "What are you doing here, Maverick?"

For more –
Check out Maverick: Satan's Fury MC
http://tinyurl.com/n9swn33

Reminder – Be sure to check out my pages:
facebook.com/AuthorLeslieWilder

Webpage:
www.lwilderbooks.com

Made in the USA
Lexington, KY
30 August 2019